Stone was carrying my suitcase.

I'd forgotten the impact of his good looks and solid frame. I was struck all over again by his confidence and intensity.

"Here?" he asked, pointing to a little bench at the foot of the bed.

The single word heated my chest. He didn't change the room temperature. It was more like he changed the atmosphere, electrifying it somehow.

I took a reflexive step back to give him room, taking a second to find my voice. "Sure. Yeah. Thanks."

He placed the suitcase on its back then turned to face me.

His bright blue eyes zeroed in, observant, encompassing, like the rest of the world had just disappeared and there was only me. I didn't know whether to be flattered or unnerved.

"You're smart," he said. "You have to know you've only got a couple of days to pull off whatever it is you're trying to pull off."

* * *

Midnight Son by Barbara Dunlop
is part of the Gambling Men series.

Dear Reader,

Welcome to *Midnight Son*, book three of the Gambling Men series.

When newly wealthy Sophie Crush goes looking for her long-lost cousin to share her good fortune, she has no idea she's about to find an entirely new family in far-flung Alaska. I loved the chance to showcase my home in the far north through Sophie's eyes as she experiences the wide-open spaces—from the family's wilderness mansion, to remote crystal lakes, to an upscale oceanfront resort.

Former foster child now powerful telecommunications-company executive Nathaniel Stone is suspicious of Sophie from the start. His intense attraction to her only complicates the situation. Then, as the truth comes out, Stone is put to the ultimate test—forced to choose between his longtime loyalty to Sophie's father and his undeniable love for Sophie.

I hope you enjoy the story!

Barbara

BARBARA DUNLOP

———

MIDNIGHT SON

HARLEQUIN
DESIRE

Recycling programs
for this product may
not exist in your area.

ISBN-13: 978-1-335-73543-0

Midnight Son

Copyright © 2022 by Barbara Dunlop

This edition published by arrangement with Harlequin Books S.A.

For questions and comments about the quality of this book,
please contact us at CustomerService@Harlequin.com.

Harlequin Enterprises ULC
22 Adelaide St. West, 41st Floor
Toronto, Ontario M5H 4E3, Canada
www.Harlequin.com

Printed in U.S.A.

New York Times and *USA TODAY* bestselling author Barbara Dunlop has written more than forty novels for Harlequin, including the acclaimed Chicago Sons series for Harlequin Desire. Her sexy, lighthearted stories regularly hit bestseller lists. Barbara is a three-time finalist for the Romance Writers of America's RITA® Award.

Books by Barbara Dunlop

Harlequin Desire

Chicago Sons

Sex, Lies and the CEO
Seduced by the CEO
A Bargain with the Boss
His Stolen Bride

Gambling Men

The Twin Switch
The Dating Dare
Midnight Son

Visit her Author Profile page at Harlequin.com, or barbaradunlop.com, for more titles.

You can also find Barbara Dunlop on Facebook, along with other Harlequin Desire authors, at Facebook.com/harlequindesireauthors!

For my fabulous sister-in-law, Melinda

One

"You'll just have to learn how to be rich, Sophie," my friend Tasha Gillen stated as if it was the easiest thing in the world.

We were standing on the breezy deck of a house for sale just north of Seattle. The bright blue Pacific Ocean spread out in front of us, edged by a steep slope of jagged rocks. The deck held a cozy cluster of rattan furniture with burgundy cushions, slatted teak side tables and a brick barbecue nook. Behind us, a high wall of glass fronted a lavish great room.

"What would I even do with six bathrooms?" I was single and feeling that singleness more and more each day.

Last year, my three closest girlfriends had been single right along with me. But they weren't anymore, none of them, and it was hard not to feel abandoned.

"You don't need to use them all at once," she said, her tone telling me I was being obstinate.

It wasn't on purpose, but she wasn't wrong about my attitude. "I can't see myself rotating through them."

"You're going to have guests, Sophie."

"Who? All my best friends have new lives."

Tasha, Layla and Brooklyn had all fallen in love, gotten married and relocated away from Seattle.

"You're playing the sympathy card?" Tasha chided.

"A little," I admitted.

Deep down, I was happy for my friends. I truly was. But they'd always been my support system, and my life had taken a very odd turn. I couldn't shake the feeling I was scrambling to catch up.

I'd helped create a new technology last summer. Called Sweet Tech, it produced fancy desserts for high-end restaurants. It was very successful—far more successful than any of the creators had ever imagined.

With the help of Tasha's husband, Jamie, we'd sold the patent to a Japanese company for a whole lot of money. The deal included royalties, which meant the checks just kept coming and coming. Having all that money turned out to be trickier than I'd expected.

"Poor little rich girl?" Tasha asked with a lilting laugh to her voice.

"Yes," I said.

She'd hit the nail on the head.

"I'm all alone," I complained. "I'm at loose ends. I'm bored."

I didn't have a job. I didn't feel productive. I didn't have any reason to go anywhere or do anything, and that was more than a little unsettling.

Tasha turned to gaze at the house again. "This would be a great place to be alone and bored. It's stunning."

I turned to take it in again. "I find it daunting."

"Don't be such a chicken."

"I'm not afraid of it." I wasn't—at least not exactly.

"You're intimidated by it," she said, and she was right.

"How would I even keep it clean?" Doing the floors alone would take an entire day.

"Sophie, you get people for that."

I laughed at the thought of getting "people." I mean, there was embracing the wealth, and then there was going full-on pretentious about it.

"You really do suck at being rich," Tasha said.

"Yeah? Well, it sounds like you've gone completely over to the dark side."

Tasha and her economist husband, Jamie, had tapped into some genius-like investment abilities and were making a ton of money in the stock market.

"I never said *I* had people," she said.

"You have people," I countered, certain of it.

She'd tossed the idea out way too casually to not be doing it herself.

"Okay, I have a couple of people. The point is you can afford a nice house like this. You can afford to live on the waterfront. I know you love the waterfront."

"I do." I did. And this house was pretty much my dream.

"You can do whatever you want now, Sophie. You should do it."

"But what *is* it?" I didn't quite keep the desperation out of my voice.

Sure, I could do whatever I wanted. Trouble was, I hadn't figured out what that was. And I'd tried pretty hard.

I'd donated to charity. Because if you had any kind of a soul at all, that's the first thing you did with an influx of unexpected money. Our local literacy organization, the hospital and the animal shelter were grateful for my support. They'd sent me thank-you letters and toasted me at parties.

But it wasn't a day-to-day gig. They didn't need me to help run things. And even if they did, I didn't have expertise in health care or teaching or animal care for that matter. I hadn't even had a pet since I was six and my bunny, Snuggles, died.

It was just me and my mom while I was growing up, and her job as a nurse didn't pay all that much. That meant we rented. She told me apartments were a lot easier to find if you didn't have a pet. So, Snuggles was my first and last pet.

"You're not going to find a small house on the waterfront," Tasha injected into our paused conversation. "The property is way too valuable."

Our house-hunting efforts had definitely proved that correct.

This was the tenth waterfront house we'd toured this week, and it was a showplace like all the rest. But I had to admit I really loved this one, even if I would have to draw myself a map to keep from getting lost between the master bedroom and the kitchen.

It was hard to wrap my head around the fact that I could buy it on a whim—just whip out the old checkbook and write down a number with a whole lot of zeros from a bank account with even more zeros.

"Maybe I could live in the garage suite," I said. "Rent the rest of it out to a family with five kids."

Tasha spread her arms. "And give up the deck?"

"I do love this deck."

Anybody would love this deck. It ran for sixty feet in three sections across the front of the living room, dining room, den and the master bedroom. Beneath it, on the lower floor, a giant games room opened to a patio with a pool and hot tub. You'd get shade down there on hot summer days, plus privacy.

"The place comes furnished," Tasha said.

I wasn't sure if that was a plus or a minus. "I already have furniture."

"You have a sofa, a kitchen table and a bed."

"It's a great sofa."

I thought about my comfy leather sofa—how long I'd saved up for it, how I'd thought such a fine and expensive piece of furniture would last me for decades.

That was one of the things about unexpected money. It obliterated most of your previous life efforts. I could buy ten leather sofas now, or a hundred leather sofas. Or I could just move into a place like this where a professional decorator had coordinated the sofas, armchairs, tables and everything else.

"Can you see yourself living here?" Tasha asked. "That's the real question. Does rich Sophie see herself sipping morning coffee on the deck or curled up in front of the stone fireplace reading a book?"

I could see that. Trouble was I couldn't see anything else. I couldn't just read and drink coffee for the rest of my life.

"I thought about park beautification," I said.

"Excuse me?" Tasha was clearly confused by my swing in topics.

I tried to explain. "After the charities, I thought about getting involved in the community. City beautification is a big thing right now. It turns out I can adopt a park."

"Or you could buy a house," Tasha said.

"And just stand around inside it all day long?"

"It's a house, Sophie. You do the same things as you do in your apartment right now, only better, bigger, more beautiful and very comfortable."

"You like gardening more than I do," I said, casting my

mind back to the park adoption website. "I'm really not crazy about gardening."

I did enjoy being in gardens. They were beautiful and they smelled so nice. But I didn't particularly like digging around in the dirt. I didn't see the appeal of that.

Tasha glanced over her shoulder at what served as the house's yard. "Those rocks down there look pretty low maintenance to me."

"I meant in the park."

"Why are we still talking about a park?"

"Because buying a house is the easy part. I'm thinking about what else rich people do. Now that I think of it, *you* should get involved in city beautification. You're the gardener. And you have time on your hands. You'd like the park thing."

"I'd also like the library thing."

That made sense since Tasha had a degree in library science.

"I joined the library board," she said.

"Really?" I don't know why it surprised me. It was a perfect fit.

"We're starting an outreach literacy enrichment program into elementary schools," she said.

"See, I need to find something like that."

"You will. You'll get the hang of being rich."

"Maybe," I said. I wasn't convinced. "I've got *all* this money."

Tasha smiled. "So, buy a house. Buy *this* house. I can tell you love it."

It was true. I did love it. Its size made me twitchy, but I found I didn't want to leave. I wanted to stay right here and enjoy it. I supposed that meant I should.

"And then what?" I asked.

Tasha shook her head in sympathy. She looped her arm

around me and gave my shoulder a squeeze. "It's too bad you don't have a few impoverished relatives."

"So, they could come and live with me in this big place?" I said it as a joke. But I wasn't joking.

If I had any family, I'd definitely help them out somehow. It would be great if I had siblings or cousins, or maybe some nieces and nephews who needed a good college education.

But my mom had been adopted and an only child. Her parents were dead now, and she hadn't known anything about her birth history or her adoptive parents' extended family.

On my dad's side, well, she'd told me he was a one-night stand. She'd been pretty up-front about it. He was a married pilot with the Australian Air Force.

They'd met at a hospital in Germany, where she was on a six-week assignment. He'd flown relief supplies for the UN in Bosnia and had suffered a head wound when his plane came under fire, and he was forced to crash land. His copilot hadn't been so lucky and had died.

My biological father had been far away from home, injured and despondent. My mom had comforted him in his grief. They'd spent a weekend together that she swore she never regretted—especially because it gave her me.

"Have you ever looked?" Tasha asked.

I struggled to remember the conversation thread. "Looked for what?"

"Your family."

"I really don't think there's anyone out there to find."

I had absolutely no intention of messing up my biological father's life.

Still, for a moment I pictured myself as an amateur sleuth digging into my heritage. Come to think of it, sleuthing might be fun. Maybe my rich future was in solving mysteries. I could set up a command centre in the games room. There was plenty of space down there.

"Go to one of those family history websites," Tasha said. "Take a DNA test."

It took me about half a second to decide it was a good idea.

"No harm in finding out," she continued. "If they look dangerous, you don't have to contact them."

I felt a surge of excitement. But behind it came a healthy dose of reality. Something like a fifth cousin twice removed—which was who I'd most likely find—wasn't exactly close family.

Still…

I was on a plane to Alaska—Anchorage to be precise. I was in first class because Tasha told me that's what rich people did. At first, she'd told me rich people would charter a private jet.

Seriously? First class was perfectly fine, thank you very much.

It was more than perfectly fine. It was champagne and orange juice, white linens, hot towels, delicate croissants with apricot jam and feeling guilty about the people squished into the coach seats fine.

It had turned out I had a first cousin, well a *likely* first cousin. We were a 13 percent DNA match. According to the website, that was very significant. His name was Mason Cambridge. He was thirty-five years old, born in Alaska, and he worked for an Anchorage-based company called Kodiak Communications.

I'd looked him up and found a few photos. He didn't have much of a social media presence, although the local newspapers had a few articles about him attending civic events. I was guessing it didn't take all that much to gain notoriety in a place like Alaska.

I'd found his physical address, but no phone number or email.

I knew I could probably track him down through Kodiak Communications, but I'd decided I wanted to meet him in person.

If he was going to send me packing, I'd rather have a short face-to-face conversation with my only known relative. Better that than a cryptic email or phone call brushing me off.

I knew I was taking the chance of being disappointed, of wasting a long trip. But it wasn't like I had a whole lot of other things to do with my time.

The purchase agreement on the new house wouldn't clear escrow for a few more days. And Tasha was back in LA now.

I might as well have an adventure.

As the plane started its descent, I was feeling sufficiently full, sufficiently pampered and more than sufficiently nervous about showing up unannounced at Mason Cambridge's house.

I rented a car at the airport and discovered Anchorage was a whole lot bigger than I'd expected—with a towering downtown, sprawling suburbs, plus green spaces and mountain vistas. If it wasn't for the GPS, I'd have gotten lost in the maze of streets.

The route eventually took me south of the city and soon the houses disappeared. Trees closed in from the hillsides to the east. From the west, waves from the inlet lapped the shore.

I saw a fox in the grass beside the highway. Then I saw a moose. When I saw two bears cross the road in front of me, I nearly pulled a U-turn and headed back to the airport. There wasn't much traffic on the stretch of road, and I had a momentary vision of breaking down and having the little SUV attacked by rogue grizzlies.

But then I came to a gravel road, and the GPS told me to turn. I was grateful the rental clerk had given me a four-wheel drive.

The road was smooth enough, considering it was gravel. But it was a winding climb through towering spruce, fir and birch trees. I started to picture Mason Cambridge as a mountain man with a grizzled beard and buckskin clothing.

He hadn't looked that way in the two newspaper photos. But maybe he dressed up to go to town. It was possible he spent most of his life traipsing around in the bush, only shaving and showering for monthly forays into Anchorage for supplies—I was guessing maybe beans, bacon and hardtack.

Then I crested the hill and came out of the trees. The gravel road ended and turned to smooth pavement.

I was surprised, shocked really, to see an expansive lush lawn dotted with tidy flower beds and sculpted shrubs. The odd pine tree rose around the edges, blending with the surrounding forest.

In the middle of the yard was a house so big it took my breath away.

Made of huge, polished logs with towering windows, peaked roofs and impressive stonework, it sprawled across the lawn two stories high, stretching out in two separate wings. It looked like a five-star hotel. In fact, I wondered if it was a five-star hotel. There were no fewer than ten vehicles parked out front.

I pulled in and parked at the end of the row.

It was possible Mason Cambridge lived in a hotel. It was odd, but definitely possible.

I set the brake and shut off the SUV.

I slung my purse over my shoulder and opened the driver's door, stepping outside.

There was a chill in the fresh-smelling air. A breeze caught me, blowing my hair into my face. I wished I'd thought to put it in a ponytail or a braid. It was too long to be loose in wind like this.

As a temporary fix, I raked it back and held it at the base of my neck as I crossed the parking lot.

I had to fight the feeling I didn't belong here. The place had a hushed air about it that didn't invite random interlopers. If I had to guess, I'd say it catered to the very rich and the very privileged.

I might have money in the bank now, but I couldn't pull off rich and privileged. My jeans were from a department store, and my purse had been on sale for twenty dollars. I didn't even want to think about my ankle boots. They were scuffed brown leather with low blocky heels. They'd seen a lot of miles. But I'd expected to need practical footwear in Alaska.

I owned my fair share of high-heeled pumps and sandals, but they were all back in my apartment in Seattle.

The place seemed to grow bigger as I got closer. The porch was at least thirty feet wide, five steps up leading up to an oversize set of wooden double doors.

I climbed the stairs and stared at the doors for a minute, wondering if I should knock or just walk in.

If it was a hotel lobby, nobody would hear a knock.

If it was a private home, it would be insufferably rude and probably illegal to just walk right in.

I thought about it and decided if it was a private home, the door would be locked.

That made sense.

I liked the analysis.

Conversely, if the door was unlocked, it was a hotel lobby.

I pressed my thumb on the latch.

It gave.

I pushed a little, and the door swung easily open to the entry. Beamed ceilings soared out over a beautifully appointed lobby.

I stepped inside. Beyond the entrance and beyond several groupings of cream-colored leather furniture, I took in a wall of glass that revealed amazing views. To the west, I could see over the cliffs and down to the ocean. South and east, a grassy meadow stretched for what looked like miles. I saw a fence line and squinted closer to eye brown animals dotting the grass.

"Can I help you with something?" The voice was deeply masculine.

"Yes," I said, giving myself a shake and closing the door behind me.

When I met his gaze, my heart took a funny beat and my lungs suddenly tightened in my chest.

He took a few steps toward me, looking like a jungle cat, all smooth motion and fluid limbs, with an arresting stare that was assessing me as—I don't know—prey?

He was darkly handsome with tousled hair, intense blue eyes, a Mediterranean tan and a whisker shadow covering his square chin. Tall, with broad shoulders and a confident stance, he was everything a woman might expect if looking for perfection.

His brow rose in a question. "Help you with…?"

"I…uh…"

He waited, while I felt more awkward by the second. I mean, it was maybe seven or eight seconds altogether, but they sure seemed long.

"I'm looking for Mason Cambridge," I finally said.

"Is Mason expecting you?"

"No. Is he here?"

"Not at the moment."

"But he lives here." I looked around again.

Mason Cambridge had to be very wealthy to live in a hotel like this.

It didn't seem like he was going to need my money for anything.

That was a small disappointment, but he was too old for college anyway. So, I couldn't have sponsored him in that.

"This *is* the Cambridge house," the man said.

It took a second for his words to sink in.

I felt a rush of mortification. "This isn't a hotel?" Oh, man. I'd just walked right on into a private home.

"Are you looking for a hotel?" the man asked.

"I'm looking for Mason Cambridge. I didn't mean to walk in on you. I thought…" I was looking around again and realizing this didn't really look like a hotel lobby. There was no check-in desk, no reception or bell staff anywhere.

"What do you want with Mason?" the man asked.

I wasn't about to explain myself to a stranger. "Do you know when he'll be back?"

"None of your business."

Neither of us were about to win any etiquette awards here. But I was entitled to my privacy, and I had a legitimate purpose in looking for Mason.

"If you met him at a bar—"

"I did *not* meet him at a bar." I knew who was losing the etiquette battle with that crack.

"At a party?" the man asked.

"Why does your mind immediately go there?" I challenged.

He looked me up and down. His expression told me he liked what he saw. He didn't even try to hide it.

Wow. No manners whatsoever.

"Because you're his type," the man said.

"I'm not his type." I paused. "At least... I mean... I've never met him."

The man gave a calculating smile.

"What?" I asked, puzzled.

"I'm glad to hear he doesn't have dibs." There was a glow of appreciation in his eyes.

"Seriously?"

He thought he could flirt with me?

He shrugged. "So, shoot me."

"Would you please just tell me what time Mason will be back? I'll go away and try this again later. I'll knock next time, I promise."

The man's smile widened. He was enjoying my embarrassment. "Sometime later today."

"Fine," I said.

"Where are you staying?"

The question took me aback.

"In case Mason wants to call you. You don't strike me as an Alaskan. I'm Nathaniel Stone, by the way."

"Sophie Crush. I'm not an Alaskan."

"Are you staying at the Tidal, the Mountainside?"

"I haven't decided." I supposed I could have made a hotel reservation before I left Seattle. But I hadn't considered that Anchorage would be such a hotbed of tourism that I couldn't find a place once I got here.

"Then I'd recommend the Tidal. Or if you're on a budget, the Pine Bird is nice."

I choked back a laugh at that, thinking about my recent conversations with Tasha. No, I wasn't on a budget.

"Something funny?" he asked.

I shook my head. "Not at all."

"Random laughter? I'd feel obligated to warn Mason if you're…pulling some kind of prank…"

"I'm not…pulling some kind of prank. And I'm not on a budget. I'll try the Tidal."

"Good choice. What do you want me to tell Mason?"

It was a fair question. I tried to frame something innocuous to say. But then the door opened behind me, and Nathaniel's focus moved there.

"Oh, good," he said to whoever had entered. "You're early. Mason, Sophie Crush is here to see you."

My stomach fluttered in anticipation. I took a swift bracing breath and turned to find another fit, good-looking man standing in the doorway.

"Hel…lo," he said, drawing out the word like it was a compliment.

"She won't tell me what she wants," Nathaniel said.

Mason gave a carefree grin. "I don't care what she wants." His gaze met my eyes. "The answer is yes."

I knew I had to nip this flirtatious thing in the bud. If I didn't, we were both going to be very embarrassed.

So I just came out with it. "I'm your cousin."

Mason's expression froze.

"What?" Nathaniel asked from behind me.

After my revelation, they hustled me into a private room.

I presumed it was the den, since most of the small mansions I'd viewed had dens. They tended to be decorated with bookshelves, writing tables and oversize chairs, with warm light that beamed against gleaming wood-paneled walls.

This one was no different, and Mason closed its door behind the three of us.

The ceiling was lower than in the great room—it was twelve feet high instead of twenty-four. I sat down in an armchair facing a set of windows that overlooked the pretty front yard and the forest beyond.

Outside, everything was fresh and green. The air was crystal clear, the sky blue with a few wispy clouds. I didn't see any more wildlife scampering around the lawn, but it felt like something interesting could emerge from the forest at any moment. Alaska felt surreal—like I'd wandered up to the edge of the earth.

I was sitting on one of four brown-and-butter-yellow plaid armchairs. Mason was across a low glass-topped table from me. Nathaniel was next to him.

I couldn't help checking out Mason's features and comparing them to mine.

His chin was different, square where mine was narrow. His nose was bigger, but in the ballpark of the same straight shape. His eyes were lighter brown. Mine were espresso dark. His hair was almost black, full and thick to my golden brown.

If I had to pick one thing, I'd say his lips looked familiar. There was something about the way he smiled and their shape when he talked.

"Can I get anyone a drink?" Mason asked.

"Seriously?" Nathaniel put in with an edge to his voice.

"Well, *you* sure look like you could use one," Mason said to Nathaniel. He looked to me. "Sophie? We have wine, red or white. Or whiskey if you need it."

"I'm not the one who's been shocked by the news," I said. "I'm fine. I don't need anything to drink."

"Whiskey, Stone?" Mason asked Nathaniel as he rose. "I'm having one. Personally, I am a little shocked by the news."

"Fine," Nathaniel said.

It was clear they weren't thrilled to meet me. They'd obviously had no idea that I might exist, which got me to thinking through the possible relationships.

If the genetic connection was on my mother's side, she might have been a shameful secret who was adopted out years ago and kept under wraps all this time. If it was my father's side, then maybe he wasn't an Australian air force officer. Maybe he was a black sheep that the family had shipped off to Australia years ago over a scandal. And now I was coming back to haunt his family.

The possibilities were endless, really. And some of them could be bad. It might be best for me to leave before I caused any real trouble. I didn't want to cause any trouble.

Mason dropped ice cubes into two heavy glasses. Then he poured the whiskey from a bottle at a wet bar.

Nathaniel was glaring at me.

I tried not to look back while we waited.

He seemed more disturbed by my appearance than Mason did.

That got me wondering who he was and how he fit into the family. His eyes were deep blue, and he looked nothing like either of us.

"Does the test say for sure that we're cousins?" Mason asked as he sat back down.

"She could be making the whole thing up," Nathaniel said.

"In this day and age?" Mason asked him. "It won't take long to prove it one way or another."

"She can do a lot of damage along the way."

"I don't want to do any damage," I felt compelled to say. "I thought this might be good news, fun news."

"Fun for you," Nathaniel said. "Announcing you're a long-lost cousin to the owners of the biggest telecommunications company in Alaska."

The statement took me by surprise. It was the first I'd heard about the family owning anything, never mind Kodiak Communications. But that certainly explained the huge house. It also meant nobody in the family would need my financial assistance... Ever.

I tried not to be disappointed by that. "I didn't know they owned it."

Nathaniel coughed out a laugh of disbelief.

"We can give her the benefit of the doubt," Mason said to him.

"I'm not here to cause you any grief." I said to Mason, ignoring Nathaniel.

"So, cousins for sure?" Mason asked.

"I could be your great-aunt or you could be my great-uncle based on the common DNA percentage. But given our ages, first cousins seems a whole lot more likely."

"*First* cousins," Mason said and seemed to ponder.

"That's what the report said." I didn't have anything more to add.

Maybe I should have gone for the deluxe DNA package. It hadn't seemed worth the extra cost at the time, since I was only looking for the basics.

"What report?" Nathaniel asked. "From where? Who did it? Do you have a copy?"

"Stone," Mason said in a warning voice.

"If this is a shakedown," Nathaniel said back.

I stood. "Listen, I didn't do this to cause trouble for anyone." I looked at Mason. "I just wanted to meet you. I've met you. Clearly, I'm not a happy surprise, so I'll just head on back to Seattle before—"

"Don't," Mason said.

"Mason." Nathaniel turned Mason's name into a warning.

"Please sit down," Mason said.

I found myself looking at Nathaniel. I wasn't seeking his permission, but I was gauging his mood.

His brow was furrowed, and his mouth was turned down in a frown.

Okay, mood gauged.

"Ignore him," Mason said.

Nathaniel's voice sounded strangled. "You know what this will—"

"Sending her away won't change anything," Mason said.

"We have to protect the family."

Mason gestured to the armchair behind me. "Please."

"I want to do the right thing." I truly did.

I didn't know what I'd expected to find in coming to Alaska—maybe to be greeted with open arms, to find a big, cheery extended family sitting around a kitchen table sharing pot roast, a fiftysomething aunt who baked sugar cookies, a jovial uncle who told rambling stories. I realized my imagination had a distinct Norman Rockwell bent to it.

"Sitting down is the right thing to do." Mason looked sincere.

I sat.

"My mother was an only child," Mason said. "My father only has a brother, Braxton. I take it you're in your late twenties?"

I nodded.

"Then logic says you were conceived while my uncle Braxton was happily married to Aunt Christine. That's the only way I can see where I end up with a first cousin."

"Could your mother have had a brother?" I asked Mason.

"Definitely not. She lived in Alaska her whole life. Everybody knew the family."

"A secret half brother?" I asked, covering all the bases.

"That would make you a half cousin. The DNA percentage would be different."

"Do we really need to walk through hypotheticals?" Nathaniel asked, his tone revealing frustration. "Do you want money? Is that it?"

"Stop it," Mason barked at him.

Nathaniel's suspicions revealed his own nature, since dishonest people always looked for dishonesty in others. So, mood noted and ethics noted.

"Let's find out what she wants and get on with it," Nathaniel said.

"Don't judge me by your standards," I responded.

His eyes narrowed and his jaw went tight.

"She's got you there," Mason said. Then he took a swig of his whiskey.

"I'll write you a check right here and now," Nathaniel said.

I stood. "Well, see, that's the fatal flaw in your logic. The *very* last thing I want is money."

Before I could make a dramatic march from the room, the door swung open.

I turned to see a fiftysomething man filling the opening.

He was tall with a distinguished bearing and a stern expression. He wore a charcoal blazer over a white dress shirt. His streaked gray hair was combed back from his forehead, while his face was shadowed by a short graying beard.

"What's going on here?" he asked in a commanding voice.

Both Nathaniel and Mason came to their feet.

"Uncle," Mason said with a nod.

"Hello, Braxton," Nathaniel said.

Braxton's gaze shifted to me. His eyes were just like mine—espresso dark.

"And who's this?" he asked.

Two

Braxton's penetrating gaze bore down on me. He obviously expected an answer.

"This is Sophie Crush," Nathaniel said.

There was a beat of silence in the room.

"And?" Braxton prompted, clearly looking for more information.

I thought I should let Mason take the lead. But he didn't, and the silence stretched.

"I'm from Seattle," I said, stepping forward to offer my hand. "It's nice to meet you… Braxton?"

"Braxton Cambridge," he said as we shook.

His hand was broad, slightly callused. His grip was restrained, as if he knew his own strength and didn't want to take a chance of hurting me.

"Sophie Crush," I repeated.

"She's here to see Mason," Nathaniel said.

Braxton looked past me to the other two men. "Is there something I should know?"

"No," Nathaniel quickly said.

I let my hand go lax, and Braxton let it go as I glanced over my shoulder at Nathaniel. I didn't appreciate the way he'd beat Mason to the answer, and I let my expression tell him that.

"Yes," Mason answered Braxton.

Nathaniel gave him a glare. "Can we not wait—"

"I think we've waited long enough," Mason said.

"I'm not having fun here," Braxton said in a dark voice.

"Braxton, you should sit down," Mason said.

Braxton looked me up and down. "Is she pregnant?"

"Why does everyone go there?" I asked.

Mason looked confused.

"Nathaniel thought I was your one-night-stand."

Nathaniel frowned. "I never said—"

"You *strongly* suggested," I reminded him, and he shut his mouth.

"Nobody's pregnant," Mason said. For a moment he looked like he was going to add something more, but he didn't.

"Business?" Braxton asked, voice still gruff.

"No," Mason said.

"Depends on how you define *business*," Nathaniel muttered.

"I told you this is not about money," I shot back, losing my patience. "It's not *nearly* about money." Then I calmed myself. To Braxton, I said, "This can all end in two minutes with me walking out the door and never coming back."

Braxton's complexion looked a little darker now than it had a few seconds ago.

"That's not how this is going to end," Mason said.

"She's made a perfectly reasonable offer," Nathaniel said to Mason.

"Somebody start *talking*!" Braxton all but shouted.

Another silence took over the room.

"Sit down, Uncle," Mason said.

With a huff of impatience, Braxton marched to the nearest chair.

Nathaniel dropped down next to him in the chair I'd just vacated.

I took Nathaniel's chair and Mason sat back down in front of his drink.

"Sophie is my cousin," Mason said.

"Is what she *claims*," Nathaniel finished.

"Based on a DNA test," I added so that Braxton would have the entire picture.

Braxton's gaze jumped from Mason to Nathaniel and finally to me.

It took him a moment to speak. "*Who* are you?"

"Sophie Crush from Seattle. My mom was Jessica Crush. That was her maiden name too. She never did get married. She was a nurse, trained in the military."

Braxton looked to Mason. "What *is* this? Does Xavier know about this?"

"We just found out ourselves," Mason said.

"Sophie showed up half an hour ago," Nathaniel said. "Out of the blue."

"From Seattle." For some reason I felt compelled to repeat that.

"My dad doesn't know," Mason said. "At least I *presume* he doesn't know." He looked over at me for an answer.

"I don't think he knows." At least as far as I knew, nobody did.

"This makes no sense," Braxton said. "Who…" He thought for a minute. Then his expression turned to a very dark scowl. His tone was a near roar. "She's *lying*."

That was it.

I was done.

I came to my feet and slung my small purse back over my left shoulder. "It's been—" I almost said nice "—interesting meeting you," I said to Mason.

I gave Nathaniel a curt nod.

"I'm not a liar," I said to Braxton, who was now very red in the face. "But I can see that it's better for you if I am. So, goodbye, all."

I started for the door.

"Stop!" Mason cried out, coming to his feet. "This is ridiculous. Making her go away won't change anything. If she's my cousin, I want to know."

"She's not your cousin," Braxton said.

"Are you positive?" Mason asked him.

I paused with my hand on the doorknob. I didn't have to turn around to know Braxton had risen to his feet. I could hear it in his voice.

"I was *never* unfaithful. *Ever*," he said.

"Then how do you explain Sophie?" Mason's tone was reasonable.

"She's lying, obviously," Nathaniel said.

"Stone, you don't know that for sure," Mason said.

"Well, *you* should know that for sure, *nephew*," Braxton said.

"There's a simple way to prove it," Mason said.

I turned back. "You're welcome to a copy of the DNA test. But I'm still leaving. I didn't show up here to get in the middle of a family fight."

"You *caused* the family fight," Nathaniel said.

"Shut up, Stone," Mason said.

"I'm not about to trust her DNA test," Nathaniel said.

"I can tell you 100 percent it's a fake," Braxton said.

"She can take another one," Mason suggested. "If you're

willing," he said to me. To Braxton he said, "Pick a doctor, pick a clinic. Find someone or something you trust."

Braxton's expression relaxed. He seemed to contemplate this for a second and then sent me a sly smile. "Sure." He paused, seemingly waiting for me to back down.

I was a little surprised at his confidence. Given that I wasn't making any of this up, he had to know there was at least a small chance he was going to get caught. Where was his confidence coming from?

"Okay," I said, mostly because I was warming up to Mason.

Braxton's eyes narrowed, like he was trying to guess my game.

I stared straight back. I wasn't playing any game.

"Let me talk to Sophie alone," he said.

Here it came. The bribe. But there wasn't an amount of money in the world that would buy me off. Then again, I wasn't here to ruin his life. Maybe we'd agree to pretend he paid me off, and I'd go away quietly.

It would be a shame not to get to know Mason. But the cost might be too high.

"Out," Braxton said to Mason and Nathaniel.

It took a minute for the two men to leave the room.

"Do you always order them around like that," I asked as the door shut behind them.

"What's your game, Ms. Crush?" Braxton asked.

"No game. I just wanted to meet my cousin. All I had to go on was the percentage DNA match. That's all they gave me. I didn't get the deluxe package. Maybe I should have. Maybe it would help us all understand—"

"Please, stop talking."

I did. Mostly because I didn't have much more to say, but also thinking he was one seriously short-tempered man.

He peered closely at me. "We both know how this is going to turn out."

I nodded.

"So, what do you want? What did you hope to gain?"

"Nothing."

He gave a cold laugh. "There's no point in being coy. We're alone."

I wasn't being remotely coy. "I only wanted to know."

"Know…" he asked in a lilting tone as his gaze narrowed on me. "Whether or not I'd write a check no questions asked?"

He was ridiculously far off base.

"No," I responded in the same lilting tone. "Whether or not I had a cousin." I paused. "Funny, before I got here, I wondered if Mason might need some money. I know that sounds stupid now. But I thought maybe he might have kids who needed a good education, like I could set up a trust fund or something."

"You're good."

I was getting tired of correcting his assumptions, so I didn't answer.

"I mean, you're *really* good. Cool as a cucumber. Let's do that DNA test."

"You're sure?"

There was nothing about this man's attitude that said he was prepared to find out he was my father.

My father.

I stared at him for a full minute, letting that thought sink in.

Braxton Cambridge was very likely my biological father.

Nathaniel had deputized himself DNA test coordinator, reaching out to Braxton's doctor, who he obviously trusted.

Fine by me. I'd already trusted an anonymous website that probably subcontracted to a lab somewhere offshore.

We were back in the great room now, waiting to decide our next move. Nathaniel was in a corner talking to the doctor's office. Braxton stood alone, still scowling as he sipped on a single malt in a heavy cut crystal tumbler. I'd turned down an offer to join him. It hadn't seemed very sincere. Mason seemed to be texting someone.

I looked around, taking in the decorative log beams, the three-sided, glassed-in fireplace next to the sofa grouping and the view outside through the many, many windows. The house—mansion, I supposed you'd have to call it—was magnificent. It was many times larger than any of the houses I'd viewed in Seattle.

The great room opened to a formal dining room with a dramatic oblong-shaped oak table with a patterned burl inset of red-hued swirls. The table was surrounded by eighteen upholstered, high-backed chairs with carved wooden armrests that echoed the pattern of the table.

Through a stone archway and up three stairs, I could see partway into a vast kitchen with cream-colored countertops and banks of red-toned wood cabinets.

I moved closer to the back windows and realized the brown animals in the distance were horses. A couple dozen of them, and they weren't all brown—white, black, chestnut. They looked beautiful down there dotting the huge paddock.

"He can fit us in tomorrow morning," Nathaniel said, pocketing his phone. "But it's going to take a couple of days for results."

"Just give me the address and time," I said to Nathaniel. "I'll be there."

"Nine thirty. It's at Laurel Street and East Tudor, in the Burge Medical Building."

"Great. Can you also point me to the Tidal Hotel?" I was relieved to have this initial meeting over with.

It hadn't gone at all the way I'd expected. I was tired now and hungry. And I was a little bit emotionally exhausted. All I wanted was to kick off my boots, fall back on a soft hotel bed and order up a big burger and fries from room service. I'd earned it.

Mason looked up at me from typing his text. "What? The Tidal?"

"Nathaniel recommended it."

"Stone, what are you doing recommending a hotel?"

"She didn't have a reservation," Stone said.

"She's not going to a hotel."

"Mason." There was a warning in Braxton's low tone.

"She's staying here," Mason said with finality.

"Bad idea," Stone said.

I agreed with Stone. That was unsettling. "I'm going to a hotel." I wasn't a fan of awkward situations, and this fit all the criteria of *awkward*.

"She says she's going to a hotel," Braxton echoed.

"No, she's not," Mason said. "She's family."

Stone scoffed out an inarticulate sound.

"I happen to know she's not," Braxton said.

"I happen to believe she is," Mason said, staring levelly at his uncle.

"I happen to have two functioning feet, an SUV in the parking lot, a valid credit card and free will," I said, making my move. "I'm going to a hotel."

Braxton stifled an obviously reluctant smirk.

"You don't think she's family?" Mason asked Braxton with an arch of his brow.

"I know what I did and what I didn't do," Braxton said.

Mason fell into step with me as I headed for the door. "We have empty guest rooms here. They're comfortable and self-contained." He jabbed his thumb over his shoulder. "You'll barely have to look at those two."

"It's very kind of you to offer."

"No," Mason said. "It's selfish of me to offer. I want to hang out. I'm curious about you. Uncle Braxton can go downtown and hide at the office if he wants, and Stone can fly off to check on Kodiak's infrastructure on the North Slope. But you and me, we're staying here and getting to know each other."

"She's not your cousin," Braxton said.

"She's a stranger and probably a con artist," Stone said.

"I'm not a con artist," I said back, reaching for the door handle.

"Then you know you're my cousin," Mason said, his tone quietly triumphant.

He was right. I did know that. Unless there'd been some colossal, bizarre mix-up at the DNA lab, there was a 99.65 percent chance Mason was my cousin.

"Don't you want to get you know your cousin?" he asked mildly.

I hesitated.

"Great," Mason said. "I'll show you upstairs."

"But—" I hadn't made up my mind yet.

"Stone, go get her suitcase." Mason gallantly offered me his arm. "Is your vehicle unlocked?"

I didn't take the arm. "Are you always this bossy?"

"It's a genetic thing. Aren't you bossy too?"

"This is unacceptable," Braxton said.

"I'm not bringing her suitcase inside," Stone stated.

"You'd rather show her upstairs?" Mason asked Stone.

I couldn't help but grin at Mason's antics. But I shook my head. "It's better all around if I go to a hotel."

Mason leaned in. "It's only better for *them*. It's better

for me if you stay. And it's better for you if you stay. I'm a fun and interesting guy. You should get to know me."

I believed him. And I had to admit, he had me curious.

"Stone," Mason said, obviously taking my silence as acceptance, thereby prompting Stone on the suitcase.

"Fine," Stone ground out. "But I'd like to go on the record as being opposed to this."

"Noted," Mason said.

Braxton smacked his tumbler down on a table and stalked out of the room.

"You don't know him yet," Mason said as he watched his uncle depart. "But that was a yes."

Stone scoffed out an inarticulate sound.

"That didn't sound like a yes to me," I said to Mason.

"It wasn't a no. By default, it's a yes."

"Is that how it works?" I was skeptical that Braxton meant anything remotely like that.

"That's how it works."

"He doesn't want here."

"That's not it." Mason looked my way again. "He doesn't want it to be true."

"I'm kind of sorry it is." I was. I had no desire to upend Braxton's life. He might be abrasive and grumpy, but I didn't mean him any harm.

I considered heading back to the airport and disappearing, forget taking a new DNA test. Did I really want Braxton in my life?

"Well, I'm sure not sorry," Mason said.

"It's not true," Stone said.

I couldn't keep my annoyance at him to myself any longer. "Why would I agree to a new DNA test if I knew it would come back negative?"

He gazed at me for a moment. "I'm trying to figure that out."

"The answer's not obvious?"

"It's obvious to me," Mason said.

I was still looking at Stone. "You don't want to hedge your bets here? A little bit? Even if it's just to save face later on?"

"No."

I gave a shrug. "Okay."

I wondered if he was the kind of guy to apologize when he got something wrong. He didn't look like that kind of a guy. He looked proud, determined, also honorably loyal to Braxton if I was being honest about it.

I'd obviously upended his life too. I couldn't help but wonder why.

And then it hit me. Just because he wasn't listed in the family history website, and just because his last name was Stone, didn't mean he wasn't a Cambridge.

"Are you related?" I asked him.

"To who?" Stone asked.

"Braxton, Mason, me?"

"No," Stone said in a flat tone. "No relation."

"But you live here?" I'd assumed he did from the first moment. But now it occurred to me that I might have had that part wrong.

Stone's jaw went tight. He looked offended by the question.

"He's very close to the family," Mason said. "And he's a vice president at Kodiak Communications. Plus, it's a big house. We have to fill it with somebody."

Calling it a big house was an understatement. And calling where I was standing a bedroom was a misnomer too.

It was a suite, palatial and high-ceilinged with exposed beams and banks of windows along two walls. It had a king-size four-poster bed with a thick mattress that I'd have to hop to get up on. The windowed corner held a conversation area with a sofa, two plush, cream-colored armchairs and a couple of glass-topped tables. A marble gas fireplace took up most of one wall, while a dressing and closet area led into a massive bathroom with a huge tub, a separate shower and dual sinks.

The floor was natural wood highlighted by a plush, forest green area rug. I gave in to the temptation to pull off my ankle boots, curling my toes into the thick luxury. I dropped my purse on a cushion-covered window bench and wondered what to do with myself until dinner.

There was a knock on my bedroom door.

"Come in," I called, expecting it to be Mason.

The idea of curling up in the conversation corner and getting to know him a little bit was appealing. I had questions about his father, his family, Alaska—and maybe what it was that made a guy like Stone tick, since it was easy to see Mr. Stone was going to make my stay here as uncomfortable as possible.

The door swung open.

Instead of Mason it was Stone, and he was carrying my suitcase.

Somehow, I'd forgotten the impact of his good looks and solid frame. I was struck all over again by his confidence and intensity. He made the doorway look small, and he held the suitcase as if it was a bag of feathers.

"Here?" he asked, pointing to a little bench at the foot of the bed and walking that way in obvious anticipation of my answer.

The single word heated my chest. He didn't change the room temperature. It was more like he changed the atmosphere, electrifying it somehow.

I took a reflexive step back to give him room, taking a second to find my voice. "Sure. Yeah. Thanks."

He placed the suitcase on its back, then turned to face me.

His bright blue eyes zeroed in, observant, encompassing, like the rest of the world had just disappeared and there was only me. I didn't know whether to be flattered or unnerved.

"You're smart," he said, but it sounded like sarcasm. "You have to know you've only got a couple of days to pull off whatever it is you're trying to pull off."

"Because the DNA test will come back negative?" I didn't bother hiding my own sarcasm.

"I've known Braxton for nearly twenty years. I've never seen him lie."

"Therefore, I'm the one who's lying?"

Stone didn't miss a beat. "Yes."

I caught the logical fallacy, even if Stone didn't. "Maybe he lied about being a liar. Maybe he's really good at lying."

Stone's deep voice went deeper still, menacing. "You come into his house and insult him? You have a lot of nerve."

I gave my hair a defiant toss. "I know what I know. That's all. And it's pointless to keep arguing."

He moved closer. "Just tell me what it'll take. I can help you. *I'm* the guy you want to deal with on this."

"I'm not looking for money."

He shook his head in rebuttal. "It's the only thing that makes sense."

"It's the one thing that doesn't make sense." I wanted to put a firm and final end to this line of thinking. I didn't like arguing at the best of times. I liked it even less with Stone.

I turned my back and unzipped my suitcase. My laptop was tucked under a couple of pairs of jeans, and I lifted it out.

"Showing me your bogus DNA results is not going to help," he said.

"I'm not showing you the DNA results."

It was a beat before he spoke. "Then what are you doing?" He sounded genuinely curious.

Balancing the laptop on one arm, I booted up and called up the East Sun Tech website.

I heard, then felt Stone move to look over my shoulder. My finger faltered on the trackpad. I could feel his heat, smell his outdoorsy scent. His nearness made my skin tingle in a wholly unfamiliar way.

I gave myself a shake and clicked on the link.

"There," I said as the picture came up.

"What's this?" His arm brushed mine and the tingle increased a thousandfold.

I had to struggle to keep from sounding breathless. "That's what we sold. To East Sun Tech. Me and my friends."

He lifted the laptop from my arms for a better look.

I let it go.

"I don't get it," he said.

"I used to work in a restaurant." I shifted so I could look at him.

He seemed puzzled.

"East Sun Tech sells it now. Through suppliers and distributors all over the world. We get royalties." I could see that he still didn't understand. "Money, Stone. Lots of money. They send it every month, and I don't know what to do with it all."

I wasn't sure why I'd added that last part. Except that it was true. It's what had brought me here, so the thought that Stone could offer me a bribe to make me go away was laughable.

"You're rich?" he asked.

I took my laptop back. "I'm…" I was about to say *com-*

fortable or use some other euphemism for wealth. "Yes," I admitted. "I'm rich."

I set the laptop down on the little bench.

"Then what's this all about?" he asked.

I straightened, uncomfortably close to him now, barely six inches from his chest. It was unnerving, but I refused to be the one to back off.

We stared each other down.

His eyes went from sapphire to cobalt, and his voice lost its edge. In fact, he sounded puzzled. "What are you after?"

I thought about the answer to that. I hadn't found what I'd expected in Alaska, not by a long shot. But I was here, and now there was something I wanted.

"The truth," I said.

"Well, isn't that noble of you." With every breath, he seemed to get just a little bit closer, daring me in some way.

I lost the thread of my response.

He leaned in another inch, and my focus locked on his lips.

They were sexy lips. Sexy lips and a sexy man in a sexy room.

This time, I was the one who moved closer, tipping my chin, tilting my head. I wasn't doing it on purpose. It was just happening.

The air was still and woodsy crisp. The room was silent, not a whirr, not a buzz, completely silent.

Stone brushed my cheek with the pad of his thumb.

I closed my eyes and let the sensation rush through me, down my neck, over my breasts through to the pit of my stomach.

Oh, wow. All that from a touch?

I sucked in a breath, and his lips touched mine, closing over me, moist and hot with rich hints of aged whiskey.

I kissed him back, parting my lips, coming up on my toes, snaking my arms around his neck as his hands closed over my waist.

It was a sexy kiss, a fantastic kiss. His mouth was tender, mobile and skilled. When his tongue touched mine, I moaned. Desire bloomed in my core, flowing into my limbs.

He broke the kiss for a heartbeat, then came back, deepening it, curving our bodies together, his firm chest coming flush against my breasts, his thighs intermingling with mine.

I wanted to tear off our clothes and tumble onto the bed.

I was giving it serious thought, when a bang sounded in the hallway.

I froze.

He pulled back a little and so did I.

We both blinked at each other.

"Uh…" I started, struggling to catch my breath, not knowing what my next word would be.

"I didn't mean…" He looked as baffled as I felt.

"That was probably a bad idea." I took a step back, separating our limbs and our bodies that were erotically entangled even though we were fully dressed.

"Probably?" he asked with an edge of astonishment. Then, as if he'd just remembered it was there, his hand fell from my waist, breaking our final touch. "That wasn't what I meant to do."

"You accidentally kissed me?" I shouldn't have been amused. This was absolutely not a time for amusement. I schooled my features.

"I'd planned to appeal to your sense of honor and integrity."

"By bribing me?"

"No. Bribing was plan A. Appealing is plan B."

"Oh. Okay. Well, appeal away." I waited.

"Braxton is more fragile than he seems."

My eyebrows rose in surprise. "*That's* your argument?"

"He's been hurt in the past."

I wasn't buying the story. "Other secret offspring have come back to haunt him?"

Stone's expression turned grim. "No. He lost a daughter. She was killed in a car accident along with his wife. She was his only child. She was nine."

I reframed my impression of Braxton, not completely, but a little bit. It was a heartbreaking story.

"I'm sorry to hear that."

Stone gestured up and down my body. "So, you can see why you, coming forward with this claim of yours has affected him."

"That had to have been years ago." It was tragic, but it didn't change anything about my situation. I wasn't making a false claim to manipulate Braxton.

"You never forget a child."

"You have children?" I asked.

Stone wasn't wearing a wedding ring, and he had kissed me like there was no tomorrow, but that didn't mean anything.

Stone looked shocked by the question. "No."

"Then you're not exactly an expert." I wasn't hardhearted, but I also didn't want to walk out before I learned the truth, whatever it might be.

I didn't want to walk out on Mason either. Whatever Braxton might be feeling, Mason had made his perspective crystal clear.

Stone looked affronted. "It doesn't take an expert to know people love their children."

I couldn't argue with that, so I pivoted. "You don't think

Braxton deserves the truth? You don't think I deserve the truth?"

"I think you already know the truth, and I think Braxton deserves to be left in peace. If money won't do it, then tell me what will."

"Nothing. I'm here. I'm taking the DNA test. It'll show what it shows."

Stone searched my expression for a long time, clearly trying to figure out what made me tick.

I wanted to ask him what he saw, but he turned and left.

Just as well. There was a whole lot of volatility between us, and the situation didn't need any more complications.

Stone avoided me for the next two days. Braxton did the same. Mason was a gracious host, although he was busy working a lot of the time. Our conversations were shorter than I'd expected and hadn't moved much past polite chitchat.

I knew he'd attended college in California, and his sister, Adeline, was still in Sacramento at Cal State working on a PhD in urban development. His younger brother, Kyle, was in Alaska but off visiting some smaller communities in his job with Kodiak Communications. So I had two more cousins—well, if things turned out as expected.

As the hours and days went by, I tried to forget about kissing Stone. I wasn't very successful, especially when I caught glimpses of him coming and going.

To distract myself, I wandered down to the horses. Mason had told me the family had a sideline, leasing horses out to wilderness tourism operators. It was a holdover from their great-grandfather, and a good use of agricultural land, which was in short supply in Alaska. There were also tax breaks, apparently. I just thought the horses were beautiful. Oddly, I missed Snuggles all over again and thought

I might like to get a pet for my new house in Seattle. Not a horse, but maybe a puppy.

On the third afternoon, the DNA tests were finally delivered to the mansion.

Braxton still seemed convinced he'd be vindicated.

I considered the possibility there was a liquor-fueled hookup in his past that he'd honestly forgotten all about. I also wondered why my mother might have come up with such an elaborate story about my biological father being a married soldier from Australia.

Maybe she didn't want me to go looking for Braxton. Maybe there was a really good reason for that. Yet, I'd shown up in his life anyway. I hated to think Stone might have been right. Maybe I should have walked away that very first day.

It was too late for that.

We'd assembled in the den, door closed, wet bar at the ready.

I caught Stone's gaze on me and looked away. I wasn't quick enough to keep our kiss from blooming in my mind or to stop a rush of heat blasting over the goose bumps on my skin.

We each sat in one of the plaid chairs around the square coffee table.

Braxton watched me closely as he sliced open the sealed manila envelope. "You want to make a dash for the door?"

"I'm good." If there'd been an honest mix-up and I was totally wrong, I'd apologize, head back to Seattle and chalk this up to a very weird life experience.

It would mean I didn't have any blood relatives, at least none I'd be able to find. But I could deal with that. I'd be taking possession of my new house in a few days. I could visit some local dog breeders and spend some time deciding on a puppy.

Braxton pulled out a sheaf of papers and started to read aloud. "Results of DNA test…blah, blah, blah." He was clearly scanning his way down the top sheet.

Then he stilled.

His expression changed.

He blinked.

"Uncle?" Mason prompted.

Braxton looked at me. "It's impossible."

Stone rose like a shot and walked behind Braxton to look over his shoulder.

He looked at me. "How did you…"

"So, it's true!" Mason was obviously delighted.

"This isn't *right*," Braxton bellowed, his face going ruddy. "I did *not* cheat on Christine. Not *once*. Not *ever*. I *loved* my wife."

"It's in the past, Braxton," Mason offered.

"It's *not* in the past," Braxton said. He peered suspiciously at me.

Stone was looking suspicious too, like he thought I'd somehow messed with the results. For such a great kisser, he could sure be a jerk.

"I don't even know what lab they sent it to," I answered Stone's unasked question.

"Good grief," Mason said. "She didn't fake the test."

Braxton flipped the page, reading further. "There has to be an explanation."

"A party?" I asked, voicing the best idea I'd come up with.

He glared at me.

"Maybe when you were young, something you don't remember?"

"Don't you dare suggest I cheated on my wife in a drunken stupor."

I realized how it sounded. "That's not what I…" Well,

it was what I'd meant. But there were a limited number of explanations here.

"Were you ever injured?" I asked. "Medicated? Were you in the military? My mom was a nurse."

"I was *not* in the military. I was *not* medicated out of my mind. I am fully aware of every hour of my life thus far. I *did not* cheat." Braxton rose from his chair and slapped the DNA results down on the table.

"What about a relative," Stone asked. "A secret brother or half brother somewhere who—"

"It says I'm her *biological father*." Braxton headed for the bar.

If someone offered, I thought I would take a drink this time, wine, beer, bourbon—anything really.

"A twin?" Stone asked.

Mason sounded highly skeptical. "A secret twin?"

"Could happen," Stone said.

"Sometimes the right answer is the obvious answer," Mason said.

Braxton turned. "Are you calling me a liar?"

"I'm pointing out that the scientific evidence says you're Sophie's father," Mason said. "And Sophie's a wonderful young woman. I want you to stop and think about that for a minute."

Braxton looked confused.

"Uncle. You have a daughter."

Braxton's horrified gaze went to me.

Mason kept talking. "However it happened, whatever the explanation. *You have a daughter.*"

"I'm sorry," I told Braxton. I truly was. Right now, I wished I'd never come to Alaska.

Stone was right. I might not know Braxton's story, but he was obviously desperate to have it stay a secret. And, looking back, my mother had tried to help him.

I needed to respect what she'd tried to do. I came to my feet. "I'll get out of your way."

"Oh, no, you don't." Mason rocked to his feet and reached out, linking his arm with mine and sidling up. "I have a say in this too."

"I didn't mean for it to happen like this," I told them all. "Don't worry. I'm not going to say a word to anyone."

"But it did happen," Braxton said. "There's no stuffing the genie back in the bottle."

"I'm going to figure this out," Stone said with determination.

"I've never been that drunk," Braxton said as he tossed back a couple of fingers of something amber. But he looked more bewildered than angry now.

He poured himself another.

"Kyle will be home tomorrow," Mason said. "And we have to call Adeline."

"Whoa," Stone said. "Let's not get ahead of ourselves."

"We're not ahead of ourselves," Mason said, pointing to the DNA results on the table. "It's been confirmed."

"It doesn't have to leave this room," I said. "I can catch a flight back to Seattle and—"

"Haven't we been through this already?" Mason asked me. "You're staying."

"That was only while we waited for the results."

"I'm not giving you up just yet." He waved a hand in Braxton's and Stone's direction. "Forget about those guys. You're my newfound cousin. This family's not so huge that we can afford to ostracize one of its members."

Despite the complexity of the statement, Mason's words warmed me. Since my mother's death, I hadn't had a single blood relative. Whatever happened after this, I felt like I'd always have one in Mason.

I swallowed. "Thank you."

Stone's expression faltered.

"You should stay," Braxton said.

Stone looked at Braxton in shock. *"What?"*

Braxton didn't bother repeating himself.

"What will you tell everyone?" Stone asked.

"We don't have to tell them anything," Mason said.

"Maybe you could come to Seattle for a visit," I said to Mason. If he came to me, we could get to know each other without causing local gossip.

"Did you ever donate to a sperm bank?" Stone asked Braxton.

Braxton drew his face back in a grimace. *"No."*

"Just considering all the possibilities."

"These two are not going to chase you out of Alaska," Mason said to me. Then he paused. "Wait, do you have a job to get back to?"

I found myself locking gazes with Stone.

Then I shook my head. "No. The world pretty much spins without me right now."

"Perfect," Mason said. "You can meet Kyle tomorrow."

Three

Kyle turned out to be a near carbon copy of Mason. He was a year younger, a little taller and a little less polished, but had essentially the same features.

"Wow," he said, reaching out to touch my shoulders. "Look at you?" Then he pulled me into an encompassing hug. He rocked me back and forth in his arms, laughing.

I was shocked at his exuberance, but I managed a light hug back.

He drew away to gaze at me again. "I can't believe you even bothered with the test. She looks exactly like Braxton."

"No, she doesn't," Stone said, frowning where he was sitting at a big central island.

We were in the kitchen making fancy morning coffee at an elaborate machine built right into the wall. A basket of fragrant scones was set out on the counter. The sun was high and had been up since the two-hour twilight ended around three thirty this morning. I was glad for the black-out curtains in my bedroom.

"That's because you're not looking for it," Kyle said. He cocked his head sideways. "Get a load of that beautiful mouth."

Stone's frown deepened.

"Braxton doesn't have a beautiful mouth," Mason said from his perch at the central island.

"Sophie has the beautiful version," Kyle said.

He crossed to the coffee maker, where Stone was retrieving his full cup. "So, did we offer her a job?"

"She doesn't need a job," Stone responded.

"I won't be staying that long," I told Kyle.

"We're still hashing that part out," Mason said, taking a sip of his mocha.

"I just bought a new house in Seattle," I said as Kyle punched the buttons on the coffee machine.

It was new news to Stone and Mason, and they both looked over at me in surprise.

"It's right on the water, and I'm really looking forward to getting moved in." I carried on talking to Kyle, ignoring their stares, Mason's curious and Stone's still suspicious. "I'm moving out of my apartment, so the extra space will be great."

I wanted Stone to know I had a good life outside this newly found biological family.

"I'm going to get a puppy," I added for good measure.

"You seem almost as chatty as me," Kyle said as he lifted his brimming cup of what looked like a smooth latte.

"Not usually," I said.

He raised a brow. "That wasn't a criticism. I was thinking it must be genetic, *cuz*."

I smiled at that. I couldn't help it. Kyle was easy to warm up to. "Why don't you tell me about you?"

"Happy to. Middle child, as I'm sure you know. I work for the family firm. I head up operations. Stone takes care of technical. And Mason's client relations."

I hadn't known their exact positions in the company, so that was interesting.

"I just got back from the Kodiak Communications facility in Juneau," Kyle continued. "Hey, Stone, you should get them to walk you through the new security infrastructure. It's amazing."

"I saw it a few times under construction," Stone said.

"Well, it's a sight to behold now that it's operational. Fly over in the Cessna. You'll be home by dinner."

"I told Kirby I'd give a hand moving the horses," Stone said.

"For Radcliff Tours?" Mason asked.

Stone nodded. "Two dozen this year. They're booked solid."

"I'm heading to the lower forty-eight for a job fair in the morning," Kyle said. He looked my way. "It's in Seattle if you want to come along."

"Come along?" I asked, confused.

"The King Air's not as fast as a commercial jet, but it's nicer to fly private. I'll be there overnight, so if you have anything that needs doing. Or you can pick up a few of your things." He looked completely serious.

Kyle was offering me a flight to Seattle on a private airplane. I couldn't help thinking Tasha would be proud.

"She can buy whatever she needs here," Mason said.

"I don't need more things," I said.

"You might as well get comfortable." Kyle shrugged.

"You'll need a second pilot," Stone said.

Kyle looked surprised by that. "I can fly single."

"It's better two with crew."

"Are you hoping to abandon me there?" I asked Stone.

Kyle looked from me to Stone and back again. "What did I miss?"

"Stone's worried about Braxton," Mason told him.

"Why?"

"Have you done the math?" Mason asked his brother.

Kyle paused. He looked at me. "You mean…"

"I'm twenty-seven," I said.

Kyle's eyes widened. "Ohhh…"

"Yeah," Stone said. "Ohhh…"

"That's a surprise." In fact, Kyle looked much more than surprised. He looked perplexed. His expression told me he didn't think Braxton would cheat on his wife.

"I *am* going to figure it out." Stone folded his arms over his chest.

"It doesn't fall to you," Kyle said.

"Somebody has to step up," Stone muttered.

When the coffee chat broke up, I wandered through the cavernous house, debating Kyle's offer and wondering if I should take it and say goodbye to Mason. I'd found what I came for, and there was little reason to prolong the stay.

I ended up in a small library off the entry hall in front of a cluster of family photos stretched across the wall behind a desk. I recognized Mason and Kyle as young teenagers. The photo was taken on a trail, and they were on horseback. I guessed the man between them was their father, Braxton's younger brother, Xavier, who I'd yet to meet.

Younger versions of the two boys were in another photo of what looked like a picnic. The little girl with them on the blanket had to be their sister, Adeline.

I took another step and came to a photo of a woman and a different young girl. They were crouched in a field of wildflowers, yellows and oranges and purples. It was a bright sunny day, and they were both grinning at the camera. They had to be Braxton's late wife, Christine, and his daughter, Emily.

My breath clogged in my chest for a moment.

Emily was wearing a fancy blue dress with a matching headband over her light brown hair. Christine was beautiful, and Emily was adorable. Next was a close-up portrait of Emily, obviously taken on the same day. She was still wearing the blue headband, and the bright sunshine beamed sideways off her smiling face. Her fingertips were touching a little necklace.

I moved closer. The necklace charm was the stylized letters *EC* inset with what looked like little diamonds in the gold. Emily, for sure. I took in her eyes, her nose, her chin. I could swear there was something familiar about her.

It hit me hard then. She was my half sister.

My chest got tighter still, and my throat thickened with emotion. If she'd lived, I would have had a half sister. That would have been wonderful.

"There are photo albums somewhere." Stone's voice came from behind me.

I swallowed the emotion, not yet trusting my voice.

Stone stood beside me, looking at the pictures. "I still can't believe he's lying."

I looked up at him. "So, I must be lying."

He gave a shrug to that. "I can't see what you'd be lying about."

I supposed that was the closest he'd come to saying he'd been wrong. I couldn't see any reason to belabor the point. So I turned my attention back to the photo in front of me.

"Emily looks really happy here."

"She was a happy kid. It was a few months after this was taken…" He reached out to brush his finger across the glass.

"That she died?" I knew she'd died when she was nine, and she looked to be about nine in the photo.

"This was her birthday," he said. "August 15."

The strangest feeling washed over me, like a breeze through the still room that blew straight to my bones. "That's—" I couldn't finish.

Stone waited a moment. "What?"

I could feel his gaze on me, and I looked up. I had to force out the words. "My birthday is August 15."

We stared at each other in silence.

"You're twenty-seven," he said.

I nodded.

"Emily would be twenty-seven."

I struggled to process the information. It meant something, something huge and unfathomable.

I leaned in and looked more closely at the photo of Emily. She still looked familiar.

"Where were you born?" Stone asked in a hushed voice.

It occurred to me then. Emily had my mother's eyes. She had my mother's smile.

"Not here," I said. I shook my head hard. I couldn't accept what we were both thinking. "My mom was working on a military base in California, north of San Francisco."

It was another beat before Stone responded. "Emily was born in California."

"No." I took a step back from the photo.

"You're Emily," Stone said on a note of amazement.

"No," I repeated.

"And Emily was you."

"That can't happen." I felt angry with him for saying it out loud. "It couldn't happen. It didn't happen."

"Sophie."

"No! My mom was my mother. I was her daughter." My hands started to tremble, and my knees felt weak.

"Are you—"

I closed my eyes and swayed.

He braced my shoulders with a strong arm. Seconds later he was wrapping me in a hug, a firm one, like he thought I might collapse or bolt or something.

I didn't fight his support. I scrunched my eyes closed and buried my face in the crook of his shoulder, wanting to shut out the world and hide in the dark just as long as I could.

But I couldn't hide from my own thoughts. They boomed.

"This isn't happening," I whispered. My throat had closed in, and my voice sounded raw.

"It's going to be okay," he said.

"It can't be true. There are protocols, security features, fail-safes." From what I knew of modern hospitals, it was all but impossible to mix up babies.

"It explains the paternity," Stone said.

"It erases my *life*."

"No, no, no," he said. "You're still you. You'll always be you."

I didn't feel like me. I suddenly didn't feel like anyone. "You don't know anything about me." I was angry with Stone, mostly because he was available.

"You're right," he said. But he continued to hug me close.

I leaned into him like an anchor.

"Hey, Sophie, I wanted—" Mason cut off the words.

I opened my eyes and looked to the doorway.

Stone turned his head too.

"What are you…?" Mason asked, his voice baffled as he took us in.

Stone looked down at me, a question in his eyes.

I nodded. This wasn't something I could keep a secret.

"We need to talk to you," he said to Mason.

"What the *heck* is going on?" Mason asked. He took in my stricken expression, and his frown deepened. "Stone, if you did something—"

"I *didn't*," Stone said. "Can you close the door?"

Mason closed the double doors behind himself, still peering suspiciously at Stone.

I thought about speaking up in Stone's defense. But I didn't trust my voice.

His arm at my waist, Stone guided me to a chair at a square table.

"Talk," Mason said to Stone. His voice had a hard edge.

"We just figured something out," Stone said, sitting as well.

Mason watched me closely, looking worried.

"It's shocking," Stone warned. "You should sit down."

"Spit it out," Mason said.

"It's Emily and Sophie."

Mason's gaze shot to Stone at the mention of Emily's name.

My heart thudded hard in my chest. The more Stone talked, the more real it felt.

"They were born on the same day," he said. "Both in California."

Mason didn't react.

Stone waited for a moment, and then Mason's eyes widened to round.

"They were switched at birth." Stone's voice was low and serious.

"We don't *know* that," I blurted out.

"We do know that," Stone stated with certainty. "It's the only explanation that makes sense."

Mason stared at me. "You're Emily?"

"No!" My answer came out more sharply than I'd intended.

"She's still Sophie," Stone said. "But the genetics aren't what we all thought."

Mason dropped into a chair. "Wow."

My mind started racing with the implications. I wanted to talk to my mother. I wanted to hug her. I wanted to tell her how much I loved her, and that I didn't care what some stupid DNA test said.

Then I wanted to call the hospital and demand their records so I could figure out who had made such a colossal mistake. They deserved to answer for what they'd done.

And then the worst hit me, the terrible truth.

It should have been me all those years ago. I should have been in the car with Christine on that icy road. I should have been the one to die.

"Emily should be here," I said awash in guilt.

Both the men looked at me in confusion.

"I should be dead."

"Don't, Sophie," Stone said, reaching out his hand.

I resisted the urge to take it.

"You can't think like that," Mason said. "It was a horrible, horrible mistake."

I rose from the chair and walked back to the picture on the wall. I looked at Emily's eyes, her smile, the little cowlick in the front of her hair.

My mother, my wonderful, funny, compassionate, intelligent mother, never even got to meet her baby daughter. Instead, she got me.

I felt Stone's broad hands close around my shoulders. "It'll be okay," he said softly.

It didn't feel like it was going to be okay.

"We have to tell my uncle," Mason said from where he was still seated.

"Tell him what?" Braxton's voice interrupted.

I turned to see his imposing form fill the doorway.

Mason came to his feet. "We think there's been a mix-up," he said to his uncle.

Braxton's attention went to me. "She confessed, did she?"

"No," Stone said.

Braxton took a few paces toward us. "How'd you do it? *What* did you do?"

"Uncle," Mason said in a pleading tone.

"Don't uncle me. I deserve an explanation."

"You do," Stone said.

I knew I should speak up, but my throat hurt, and I didn't have the first idea of where to start.

"So?" Braxton said, coming to a halt a few feet away, eyeing me up and down like I'd turned right back into the enemy again.

"Sophie is Emily," Mason blurted out.

I wished people would stop saying that. It physically hurt me to hear those words.

Braxton's expression went blank.

"Switched at birth," Stone said, obviously deciding to throw it right out there.

Another beat of silence passed.

"No," Braxton said. He vehemently shook his head. "No."

I empathized.

His reaction was the same as mine.

His precious Emily was obviously as important to him as my mother had been to me. It was horrifying to have that suddenly ripped from your life.

"She's not!" Braxton said, staring at me with a cold accusation.

He seemed to think it was my fault.

Maybe it was my fault. I mean, I couldn't have stopped myself from being switched in the hospital, but I could have stayed away from the family history website. And when I learned how upsetting my existence was for Braxton, I could have walked away. I could have pretended to be a con artist so the Cambridge family could go right back to normal.

"They have the same birthdate," Mason said. "They were both born in California. And you made it abundantly clear you didn't cheat on Aunt Christine."

"No," Braxton repeated, but there was less power in his denial.

"I'm sorry," I managed.

"Don't do that," Stone said to me. "This screwup had nothing to do with you."

"It had everything to do with me. Why didn't I just stay quietly in Seattle?"

"That wouldn't have changed anything," Mason said. He moved closer to Stone and me. "It wouldn't have changed a thing. Besides, we're your family. There's no question that you belong here."

I didn't belong in Alaska.

I stood alone on the Cambridges' back deck, gazing out at the horses and the surrounding wilderness. I wasn't sure I belonged anywhere.

I felt an urgent desire to go home. But home was my apartment, and I'd already given up the lease. The movers had started packing and would unload the moving boxes at my new house in just a few days. I couldn't go back now.

At least I'd have my own things in the new house, my keepsakes and my photos. I was going to pull out all my childhood albums and photo collections and stare at them for a few hours to remind myself of my mom and my life.

The breeze freshened around me. It was midafternoon now, high summer, and the sun was doing a lazy circle in the sky. It was never straight overhead I'd discovered, but it never quite set either. The north felt like an alien world. It was impossible to wrap my head around the idea that I might have grown up here instead of in metro Seattle.

I thought about going to visit Tasha or Layla and Brooklyn in order to feel normal. Better still, I could get them all to meet me somewhere. I was sure they'd do it, especially if I told them what had happened. They'd rally around me if they knew.

A spa would be nice—a girls' weekend at the spa like we used to do, mineral pools, massages and pedicures—and wine, plenty of wine.

I heard the French doors open behind me.

I didn't turn. I didn't care who it was. In fact, I hoped if I ignored them, they'd go away. I didn't really want to see anyone right now.

"Sophie?" It was Braxton's voice.

I tried to steel myself, but I wasn't remotely ready for whatever he might have to say. My emotions were too close to the surface, and I didn't trust myself not to tear up.

He came up to the railing a few feet away from me and leaned against it.

A horse whinnied in the distance. Chickadees chirped from the trees as a gust of wind rustled the poplar leaves and a few fluffy clouds inched their way across the clear sky.

"You okay?" he finally asked.

I almost laughed at the question, partly because it was so absurd, and partly because Braxton's gruff, guttural voice made it sound like he resented having to ask at all.

I wondered if Stone and Mason had forced him to come out here and talk to me.

I faced him, bracing my hip on the rail. "You don't have to do this."

"Do what?"

I waved my hand toward the house and the people who'd obviously sent him. "Pretend you care."

He took a step closer to me. "You don't think I care?"

"Why should you care? I'm a stranger. We're strangers."

His bushy brow went up. "You're my daughter."

"No, I'm not." I let out a chopped laugh. "I mean, I am. But I'm not."

His deep chest rose with an indrawn breath. He was a sturdy man, tall with broad shoulders and a very deep chest. His striking presence had me thinking about genetics.

I was sturdy, slim, but not fine boned. And I'd always been more athletic than my mom. I'd assumed I got it from my dad. Which I had. I knew that now.

"Right." His flat response resonated in the big outdoors.

I didn't know where we were supposed to go from here. I had no interest in a heart-to-heart talk with a callous stranger. I hadn't even wrapped my own head around this reality.

But he didn't leave, and the silence was growing less comfortable by the second.

"Did Stone and Mason make you do this?" I asked.

"Do what?"

"Come out here, talk to me, make…I don't know, a connection or something."

Braxton gave a ghost of a smile. "No."

I digested that for a moment, not sure whether I believed him. I decided to let it slide. "Okay. So, what do you want?"

"Believe it or not, to see if you were all right."

"In what way?"

He shrugged his wide shoulders. He was clearly uncomfortable, and I had to give him credit for sticking it out this long. I wasn't making it easy.

"I thought you might be upset," he said slowly, as if he was feeling his way through the statement. "Maybe angry? Confused?"

"Confused," I said, finding something to agree with him on. "Definitely confused."

He gave a nod. His voice went lower, quieter. "Me too."

We gazed at each other for a long minute.

Braxton broke the silence. "I can see Christine in you now."

I wasn't sure I believed him. Only a few hours ago he was disavowing me, and now he could see the family resemblance?

"I wasn't looking for it before," he said, as if he knew what I was thinking. "I hope you understand why I wasn't looking. I knew with absolute certainty that I wasn't your father."

Truth was, I did understand his perspective now. There hadn't been a drunken party in his past, no injury with mind-addling pain medication that made him forget about a one-night stand with a pretty nurse. All along he'd known he was right, but I kept pressing and pressing.

Served me right for what I found out, I supposed.

"I need to go home," I told him honestly.

He looked disappointed. "If that's what you want."

"I have a life out there." I thought again about Tasha, Layla and Brooklyn. They were the closest thing I had to family since my mom died.

"You could stay a little longer," Braxton said, sounding almost hopeful.

I shook my head. "I need to get my feet under me, get centered, think about what all this means."

"You could do that from here."

I needed something familiar, something from my past to cling to while I reframed my world. I'd come to Alaska hoping to find a cousin. Instead, I'd lost my mother.

"You expected to find family here," Braxton said.

"Not like this." I took a shuddering breath, struggling to control my emotions. "She was my *mother*."

Once again, the outdoor sounds echoed around us under the massive sky.

"I had one child." Braxton shifted his focus to the horizon, and his voice sounded far away, drawing my sympathy. "My wife, Christine." He swallowed. "I mean, your mother."

Something twitched inside me and wanted to erupt in a protest. Christine couldn't usurp mother, not so easily, not just like that.

"She nearly died giving birth to Emily." Braxton seemed to gather himself. "I mean to you. Her blood pressure skyrocketed, and her kidneys very nearly shut down. After that…well, we didn't dare have another child. But then I lost them both. It was so sudden, and they were both so young." He turned his head, and his eyes focused on me. "But here you are. Here…you…are."

"I'm not her." The world shifted beneath me, rolling like I was on the deck of a ship, and I gripped the railing.

"But you're you. And that's something. That's some kind of a miracle."

I didn't want to be a miracle. I didn't want that at all.

I only wanted my life to be mine again. The one I recognized.

I was packing.

I'd taken Kyle up on his offer of a ride to Seattle, and I didn't know when I'd come back.

I'd call Tasha as soon as I got home, because I was

liking the spa idea more and more. I wanted to mentally check out from reality, somewhere warm and cozy with my dear friends and skilled massage therapists and a well-stocked wine cellar.

Maybe we could try Vegas again. Layla's and Brooklyn's husbands owned an elegant hotel on the strip. We could probably get a discount. Not that money was an object anymore.

There was plenty of space in the dresser drawers and closet in the guest room, but I'd been living out of my suitcase. I hadn't felt like I should settle in. Turned out I was right.

Now I dumped everything onto the bed and started re-sorting and folding.

Over my objections, Marie, a superfriendly fiftysomething housekeeper had taken some of my shirts and underwear away to wash them. I'd asked her not to bother, to just point me to the washing machine, but she'd laughed and told me to act like a guest, not a staff member.

I hoped she'd have them done before it was time to leave. If not, well, I figured I'd buy new ones when I got back to Seattle. At least it would give me something to spend some money on.

There was a knock on my open door.

"Yes," I called out.

I doubted it was Braxton. It would be ironic if it was Marie. But my money was on Mason. He'd probably talked to Kyle by now and wanted to convince me to stay.

I didn't want to hurt his feelings, but he wouldn't change my mind.

"You're packing." It was Stone who walked in.

"I'm packing." I confirmed the obvious, tucking a pair of jeans in next to my tennis shoes.

I wondered if Stone was still thinking about copilot-ing the plane with Kyle. I hoped not. It would be better to walk away from him here than be cooped up together in the air for a few hours and then say an awkward goodbye in Seattle.

Though we were both trying our best to ignore it, our kiss hung between us. I could tell by the way he looked at me, as if he was searching for an answer to a question.

I also couldn't forget how his arms felt around me in the den in those minutes after we'd discovered the baby switch. He'd been compassionate and comforting. I wouldn't have guessed he had something like that in him.

"You're leaving." His tone made the statement into an accusation.

"That's why I'm packing." I lifted a T-shirt from the bed only to realize two pairs of my panties were beneath it. I set it back down again.

It was silly, but I didn't really want him staring at the filmy silk and lace. He didn't need to know I liked mint green and pale blue.

"Braxton said he asked you to stay." Stone came farther into the room.

I turned to face him, ready to stand my ground but also protecting my privacy by blocking his view. "I prefer to leave."

He frowned. "Are you sure that's the best idea?"

"For me? Yes."

He looked like he was about to mount an argument.

I preempted him. "Come on, Stone. You've been desperate to get rid of me since I first showed up."

"He wants you to stay."

"I know."

"He doesn't ask for much."

I blinked in surprise. "Seriously? Braxton strikes me

as a guy who asks for and gets everything his own way, always."

"It's a facade."

"I don't think so." I turned back to what I was doing.

Forget about hiding my undies. Whatever Stone saw, he saw.

He touched my shoulder. "Sophie."

I froze. The gentle pressure sent magnetic waves of warmth along my arm, down into my chest.

"It's my decision," I managed.

"Will you hear me out?"

I fought the urge to turn in his arms. "This isn't about you and me."

Silence followed my words.

"It can be," he said.

"Stone."

"Do you want it to be? Am I the reason you're leaving?"

I turned and his hand fell away from my shoulder. I missed it. No, I didn't. *Yes*, I did.

"*I'm* the reason I'm leaving."

"I know I wasn't as welcoming as I could have—"

His words surprised a laugh from me.

He frowned. "To be fair, I thought you were a con artist."

"To be fair, I'm not. You could have given me the benefit of the doubt at several points during the past few days."

"*That's* how people get conned."

The reaction gave me a peek into his psyche. "What happened to make you so cynical?"

"I was in foster care." His bald statement took me by surprise.

I didn't know what to say.

"You learn to be suspicious," he said.

"I...had no idea."

"Why would you?"

"I'm sorry." It sounded like a difficult way to grow up.

"Five foster homes in ten years. I'm not saying that to get your sympathy. Though I'll take it if it helps you stay." His self-deprecating quirk of a smile was disarming.

"Don't try to charm me," I warned him.

"Is it working?"

"No." I wasn't going to let it work.

"I met Braxton when I was fifteen," Stone said, sobering. "I was on the wild side back then. My friends and me were looking for fun, and to us that meant trouble. We climbed into one of Kodiak Communications cell tower compounds."

"You got caught," I guessed.

I could easily picture Stone getting into trouble back then. It was his cocky attitude, his defiant look, like he'd always run by his own rules and nobody else's.

"Not while we were in there," he said. "But we neglected to factor in the security camera."

"Whoops."

"We were young, not particularly good at crime. We used the satellite dish for target practice."

"You had guns?" I asked in shock.

"Slingshots. I had the best aim." He paused. "Took out over a thousand customers."

"What did Braxton do?"

"That's the thing. He could have thrown the book at me. I could easily have ended up in juvie. It would have derailed my life for sure."

"He didn't?" That surprised me. Everything I'd learned about Braxton told me he didn't have compassion, didn't give second chances.

Stone shook his head. "When he found out about my history, all those foster homes, he made me a deal. I could live with him under 'house arrest' and work off the cost of the repair—a combination of laying data cable and shoveling horse manure. He said if I kept my nose clean and my grades up, he'd drop the charges."

"That was…" I couldn't find the right word: *generous, compassionate, noble.*

"He saved my life. Well, my future anyway. He gave me a home, gave me a job and funded my education. Everything I am, I owe to Braxton."

My opinion of Braxton shifted again. How could it not?

Braxton wanted me to stay so Stone wanted me to stay. Problem was, *I* didn't want to stay. And my opinion counted too.

"I've got some thinking to do," I told Stone. "I need time and space."

"Think here," he said.

"It's not—"

"There's time in Alaska. There's space in Alaska."

"I'll come back later," I said.

His look of disappointment tugged at my heart. "Why don't I believe you?"

"Because you're cynical."

He gave me another half smile for that one. "People don't always do what they say they're going to do."

"He's my father." As I uttered the words, I knew for certain I'd be back. And probably sooner than I'd planned. I very much wanted to know my biological family.

"Why waste time?" Stone asked.

It was a good question. I didn't have a ready answer.

Four

"Staying or going?" Mason found me in the kitchen the next morning.

I was an emotional eater, and Marie had pointed me to a batch of lemon cupcakes that cook Sebastian baked, saying they were fair game for all.

I'd called Tasha last night, and I was still recovering from that and everything else.

She'd been stunned to learn I was switched at birth. She'd been alternately excited and sympathetic, also endlessly supportive and reassuring. Before the long call ended, she'd helped me pro and con the situation from every conceivable angle.

"Kyle says you're going," Mason continued as he came my way. "Stone says you're staying. Who's got it right?"

I set the cupcake on a little plate and licked an errant dab of vanilla icing from my thumb. I'd been contemplating taking two—they were small—but Mason's presence made me hesitate on my splurge. I set the glass cover back on the platter.

"Staying," I said.

Mason's shoulders relaxed. "Thank goodness." He rounded the big island and helped himself to a cupcake. "I didn't believe Stone when he said he'd talked some sense into you."

"Stone said that?"

Mason nodded and bit off half the cupcake.

I slipped up onto a stool at the island and shifted my cupcake in front of me, gazing at the fluffy buttercream and the swirl of sugared lemon peel, anticipating that first savory bite. Sweets were my weakness, that was for sure.

"Stone didn't have much to do with it." I was crediting Tasha more than anyone. Then again, if I was being honest with myself, the conversation with Stone had prompted me to call Tasha in the first place—instead of just getting on the plane. "He had a little to do with it. We had an argument."

"Stone can be hard-nosed."

I smiled at the understatement. "He said he wanted what Braxton wanted."

As Mason nodded, I took a bite of my cupcake, and my taste buds leaped with joy. The cake was moist and fluffy. The icing was sweet, the lemon flavor tart.

"Oh, wow," I said with a smile. "That's delicious."

"Sebastian is a treasure," Mason said. "You should try his burgers. Stone always wants what Braxton wants."

"He told me about being a foster kid and how Braxton helped him."

"He did?"

I nodded as I took another heavenly bite.

Mason looked thoughtful. "I'm surprised. Is that what changed your mind?"

I kept the discussion with Tasha to myself. "I realized I'd just end up coming back anyway. And, I'm here now. I might as well get to know you."

Mason looked happy. "That's good. So, what do you want to do first? Need anything? We could go into Anchorage. I'll show you around the town."

"I saw some of it when we got the DNA test."

"That wasn't the best part. We can stop by Kodiak's head office. You might rethink your interest in the business."

I finished the final bite of my cupcake. "Telecommunications? Not even remotely in my area of expertise." I didn't want Mason or Stone or anyone to think I was settling in here for the long haul. "Plus, my life is in Seattle."

"Message received," he said. He took another cupcake and perched on a stool across from me. "We could still do a tour of Anchorage."

"I'd like that." It would be fun to spend some time with Mason.

"Like what?" Stone asked as he walked in.

"A tour of Anchorage," I said. "I just told Mason I'd stick around for a few days."

"Only a few days?" Stone asked.

"Don't push her," Mason warned him.

"Don't manage me," I told them both. I pointed at Stone. "You didn't persuade me." I turned to Mason. "And you won't influence me."

"Not even if I'm super charming and fun, the best cousin ever?"

"I'm not here to have fun."

"You might as well have some fun," Mason said.

A diesel engine rumbled outside the house, and its backup alarm emitted loud beeps.

Stone's brow shot up, his attention going to the window. "They've started already?"

Mason grinned at me. "You definitely have to stay for the party."

Stone shifted over to the window and looked outside.

"Party?" I craned my neck to see what was going on, but the truck was beyond my field of vision.

"A week Saturday." Mason stood to go look himself.

I followed suit.

"The annual Kodiak Communications staff appreciation party," he said as a big green-and-white semi backed its way along a narrow driveway curving beside the vast lawn between the house and paddock. "Everybody comes. We have a massive barbecue, a band and dancing, plus trail rides and games for the kids in the afternoon."

Stone opened one of the French doors, and the three of us filed out to line up on the deck, watching. I stood between them feeling, the throb of the engine and listening to the high-pitched backup alarm.

I wasn't sure how I felt about attending a company party when I wasn't part of the organization. I'd feel like an interloper.

"What's in the truck?" I asked instead of committing.

"The tent," Mason replied.

"Once it's up, we'll get the sound system, tables, stage, a dance floor."

"You're building a dance floor in your yard?"

"For the dance," Stone said.

I shot him a look of impatience, catching the twinkle in his eyes.

"Ha, ha," I said back.

"It's a great party," Mason said. "If I was you, I wouldn't want to miss it."

"Bribery's not going to work."

"This isn't bribery," Stone said. "It's an opportunity."

"What would you even tell people about me?" I wasn't planning to stay that long, but the question had me curious.

"The truth," Stone said.

"Whatever you want us to tell people," Mason offered.

The thought of Braxton's friends and associates knowing about me felt weird.

"She's not a shameful secret," Stone said.

"She's entitled to her privacy," Mason said.

"I thought we'd keep it to family for now." I considered Tasha family, Layla and Brooklyn too.

I felt a sudden urgency to reach out to Layla and Brooklyn and bring them in on everything. I reached for my phone, but I couldn't make a call out here in the noise.

I waved my phone to indicate what I was doing before turning to the house.

"Hello?" A woman appeared in the doorway in front of me.

I quickly came to a halt, feeling slightly flustered. "Oh, hello."

She looked past me, obviously to where Mason and Stone stood. "Are you visiting…Mason?"

I didn't answer. I wasn't exactly sure what to say about myself.

"Stone?" she tried again, looking surprised by that.

"Neither," I said. "Well, both." I twisted my head to see if they were looking.

They were still watching the truck back up, so they didn't know we were behind them.

"I'm Adeline," she said.

I looked back in surprise. This was Adeline? I'd only seen her in childhood pictures. She'd grown up.

"Mason's sister," she added.

"I know. I'm…"

"Are you here on business? Kodiak stuff?"

"No." I looked back again, wishing either Mason or Stone would see us and join in. "It's…uh…a bit complicated."

Adeline looked intrigued. "You're with *both* of them?"

"Oh, no, not that kind of complicated."

"Adeline!" Finally, Mason's voice.

The truck engine suddenly went silent, and both Mason's and Stone's footsteps sounded on the wooden deck.

Adeline brushed past me, and I turned to see her hug her brother. Then she hugged Stone, rocking back and forth in his arms, a broad smile on her face.

"What are you doing home?" Mason asked.

"For the party," she said.

"You're early." Stone looked puzzled. He glanced over her head at me.

She linked her arm with his and turned my way. "Introduce me, why don't you?"

Stone nodded at Mason, obviously letting him take the lead.

"Adeline," Mason said in a serious tone. "This is Sophie. She's…" He looked to Stone, squinting in obvious hesitation.

"A complicated story," Stone filled in for him.

Adeline considered me with curiosity. "That's what she said."

"She's a long-lost relative," Mason said. "We have the DNA test to prove it."

"DNA?" Adeline asked.

"Sophie Crush." I stepped forward and offered her my hand.

"Cousin Sophie Crush," Mason said.

Adeline turned her head to Mason, clearly baffled.

I let my hand fall away.

Stone spoke up. "She and Emily were—"

"Sisters?" Adeline asked. "I don't get it. How does *that* work?"

"Switched at birth," Mason said. "Sophie and Emily were switched at birth."

Adeline reared back, and Mason steadied her.

"You're a girl." Adeline spoke giddily, reaching across the bistro table to squeeze my hand.

The four of us had taken a driving tour of Anchorage, walked a few streets, checked out some shops, then decided on the Moonstone Grill. The place was cozy and comfortable, with padded leather chairs and a big round fireplace burning in the middle of the room. I could feel the heat on my back.

She looked at Mason and then at Stone, who were on either side of her at the round table. *"Finally.* I've been outnumbered for years."

"Oh, you poor thing," Mason said with false sincerity.

A waitress had dropped off a round of drinks, chatting easily with Stone and Mason, who were clearly regulars. Adeline had ordered a martini, Stone and Mason a local beer on tap, and I went with a glass of merlot.

"You have to tell me everything," Adeline said to me.

It was easy to warm up to her. She was bubbly and friendly, insightful and funny. And her only reaction to me appearing in the family seemed to be delight.

I couldn't help smiling at her eagerness. "Everything about what?"

"What you do, where you grew up, what your family was like." She sat back in her chair. "Start at the very beginning."

"Can we order first?" Mason asked. "It could be a long story."

"We can talk and order at the same time," Adeline said.

"Sophie hasn't memorized the menu," Stone said.

"Get the pesto quesadilla," Adeline told her.

"You don't know what she likes," Mason said.

"Do you like yam fries?" she asked.

"I do," I answered.

She looked at her brother. "Who doesn't love chicken and pesto?"

"Someone with tree nut allergies."

I stifled a smile at their good-natured bickering. I'd watched Layla and her brother, James, do it most of my life.

Stone caught my look and rolled his eyes, grinning back.

"Sophie doesn't have allergies," Adeline asserted. "Nobody in our family has allergies." Belatedly, she looked at me. "Do you?"

"No allergies."

"See?" She nodded to Mason.

"I recommend the beluga burger," Mason said. "No actual beluga. It's beef on a homemade bun with their signature sauce."

They were both staring at me, and I felt like I was caught in the middle.

Stone opened the menu in front of me. "Maybe Sophie could choose for herself."

"I like the sound of the quesadilla," I said.

Adeline looked triumphant.

Stone arched a brow in my direction.

I wasn't staying loyal to the sisterhood. The quesadilla did look good to me. And I loved yam fries.

But I did dutifully glance down at the menu. A slice of banana cream pie instantly caught my attention. It was thick with whipped cream covered in what looked like white chocolate shavings.

"That one's my favorite," Adeline said, seeming to see where I was staring.

"So, we're having dessert?" Mason asked.

"It's a celebration," she said.

"That's champagne," he said back.

"Are either of you going to let Sophie talk?" Stone asked.

Mason and especially Adeline looked confused.

"She can talk anytime she wants," Adeline said.

"What's stopping her?" Mason asked.

"The two of you," Stone piped up. "She can't get a word in edgewise." To me, he said, "Their conversational style is an acquired taste."

Everyone stopped talking then and stared at me.

"Oh, great," I said. "No pressure at all."

"Say something brilliant." Adeline grinned.

"Tell them about your invention," Stone said.

"You have an invention?" Adeline asked.

"What does Stone know about it?" Mason asked.

"You're doing it again," Stone said with a frown.

They both stopped talking and stared at me.

"It's a dessert-making machine," I said. "I worked with some brilliant friends to create it, and we sold the patent."

"To who?" Mason asked.

"What does it make?" Adeline asked.

"Delicacies," I answered Adeline first. "Very fancy and very precise with lots of cream, ganache and pastry. We sold it to East Sun Tech in Japan."

"Japan?" Mason looked impressed.

"I didn't sell it myself," I clarified. I didn't want to take the credit. "My friend Tasha's husband has contacts all over the world. He's my other friend Layla's brother, and I've known him for years. Without him, we'd probably still be tinkering in the garage and schlepping it around to local restaurants in Seattle, auditioning it."

The waitress approached us again, thirtysomething, petite with wavy brunette hair and round flushed cheeks. "Are you all ready to order?"

"I think we're set," Stone answered.

"The usual?" she asked him.

"You bet."

She turned to Mason.

He gave her a nod. "Cheeseburger and home fries for me."

"Extra fries," she said as she made a note.

Mason smiled.

She looked to me next, her blue eyes open and friendly. "What looks good to you…"

"Sophie," Adeline supplied my name. "She's our—"

Mason swiftly nudged his sister under the table.

"—visiting from Seattle," Adeline finished smoothly.

I was impressed with her recovery. "I'd like the pesto quesadilla."

"Welcome to Alaska, Sophie. I'm Janine. You want the yam fries with that?"

"Yes, please, Janine. I'm told they're delicious."

"You got some good advice there," she said.

"A quesadilla for me too," Adeline said. "Extra guacamole if you can."

"We can," Janine said. She sent a silent question my way, obviously wondering if I'd take Adeline's lead.

"Sure," I said. "Adeline seems to be the expert."

"Got it," Janine said. "Give me a shout if you need more drinks."

"Thanks," Stone said, gathering my menu along with his own and handing over.

"You must come here a lot." I could see why they would.

The ambience was laid-back and friendly, the decor was subdued and the seating more than comfortable.

"The DJ starts at eight," Adeline said. "Dancing if you want it."

I couldn't help a fleeting glance at Stone. Then my gaze caught Adeline's and she gave me a secretive smile.

I wanted to shout out *no*. That hadn't been what I'd meant at all. I didn't want to dance with Stone. I mean, well, sure, maybe it would be fun to dance with him. Although, who knew if a guy like him would even dance? But I didn't want Adeline to get the wrong idea.

"Ladies' room?" Adeline asked me, pushing back her chair.

"Sure." Perfect. I'd clarify things for her while we walked.

"So, Stone, eh?" she said before I could even broach the subject. She linked her arm with mine. "He's pretty hot."

"No."

"What do you mean no?"

"I mean, I didn't mean that the way it looked."

"Your moon-eyes at Stone?"

I whirled to try to face her directly.

Adeline tugged at my arm, redirecting me around a table. "Watch out."

"I did not make moon-eyes at Stone," I said, fearing I might have done just that.

"It was subtle. He didn't notice."

"Subtle moon-eyes?"

She laughed as we crossed the foyer to a small staircase.

I might be uncomfortable, but I couldn't help but like her. "It's not…"

"You think he's hot." She nudged her hip against mine. "Don't worry about it."

"We mostly argue. We don't see eye to eye on anything. He thought I was a con artist when I first showed up."

She went ahead as we started up the stairs. "Because you claimed Uncle Braxton was your father?"

I followed, and the aging stairs creaked under my feet. "I didn't know that part at first. I didn't even think that at first. All I knew was that Mason was probably my cousin."

"I can't believe Mason gave them his DNA. That's weird for him. Don't get me wrong, I'm superglad he did. Otherwise we'd never have met you."

"You're not…" I tried to figure out how to phrase my question. "I don't know, mad about Emily?" I had to think that Adeline and Emily had been friends growing up. The two families seemed so close.

"That was such a tragedy," Adeline said, stopping outside the ladies' room door. "We were years getting over it. But it wasn't your fault."

"I feel like it was…like it should have been me."

"Well, it should have been you. But then we'd have been just as devastated to lose you."

I thought about that. It made some sense.

"We can't change it, Sophie."

That was true too.

"Do you need the restroom?" she asked.

I shook my head. I'd just come along for the ride.

"Me neither."

We both turned and headed back down the staircase.

Adeline paused in the reception area. "I was going to offer to help get you together with Stone."

I lowered my voice, since the hostess was watching us. "I don't want help getting together with Stone."

"Are you sure? Maybe a little dancing later."

"No."

"He really is hot."

"Stone and me, not a good idea." The attraction was there all right, but so was the combustion, the exasperation and the complications. I didn't even want to get started on the complications.

Adeline looked puzzled now. "How can you possibly know that?"

I pressed my lips together as I tried to form a reasonable answer.

"Something already happened?" The expression on Adeline's face told me she was entirely too intuitive. She pulled me into an alcove where we had more privacy.

"Nothing happened," I said. It hadn't. Not really.

"Define nothing."

"Are you always like this?" I tried to deflect.

"Like what?"

"So...so..."

"Right?"

"I didn't say that."

"But you meant it." She gave her thick auburn hair a little toss. "I have a knack."

I couldn't argue with that. "For reading minds?"

Her green eyes lit up. "So, something *did* happen. I knew it."

I decided it was stupid to keep playing this game. "I kissed him. Or he kissed me. We kissed each other."

"And...?"

"And nothing. We stopped."

"Why?"

"Because we didn't mean to do it. We were fighting. He was trying to get me to leave Alaska, and I was insisting on finding out the truth."

She looked confused. "Wait. I thought Stone talked you into staying."

"He didn't talk me into anything. I don't know why he keeps trying to take credit for it. Yes, sure, *now* he wants me to stay. But back then he wanted me to get the heck out of Alaska and never come back."

"He always takes my uncle's side. They stick together, you know." Her expression turned more serious.

"Stone and Braxton?" I assumed that's what she meant.

"All of them. The Cambridge men. They never listen to a thing—" Her expression brightened again. "But that's irrelevant. I'm here for you if you want my help."

"I don't need any help with Stone." I'd finally gotten a certain composure about my feelings for him. I wasn't going to act on them. "I'm staying to get to know Mason and you and Kyle. I've never had cousins before."

She linked arms with me again. "You're going to love having cousins. At least, you're going to love having me as a cousin. And I'm going to love having you. Be careful of the guys though."

I was surprised by her warning. She seemed to have a great relationship with her brothers, at least with Mason. I hadn't seen her interacting with Kyle yet, since he'd headed off to Seattle.

"Why?" I asked.

"They're very strong-minded."

"I'm strong-minded too."

"Just watch yourself, that's all. I bet our food's almost ready."

I found myself agreeing with Adeline about strong-mindedness as I watched Stone and Kyle directing the yard setup for the Kodiak Communications barbecue. They both seemed to know exactly what they wanted.

The Cambridges' backyard was at least five acres. The gardeners had ridden around on multiple mowers this morning, trimming everything even. And there were still at least six of them fine-tuning the garden beds close to the house. A string of six horses stood along the fence watching the goings-on.

They'd erected a massive tent with a clear top, which I thought was a very nice touch. Its sides were open, and blue draping was being hung from the peaked ceiling alongside rows and rows of little white lights. Lights and some greenery also decorated the lattice pillars that camouflaged the tent poles. I could picture the final effect in my mind. It was going to be magnificent.

I watched some of the workers unloading tables from a truck trailer. They were rectangular, utilitarian. I knew you could spruce them up with tablecloths and centerpieces, maybe some candles and decent dinnerware. But they were less than ideal, especially given the beauty of the tent itself.

I approached a man who seemed to be in charge of setting up the dining area. He was fiftysomething, stocky, with a receding hairline. He wore navy pants and a crisp striped shirt with a blue tie and his sleeves rolled up. He was checking a tablet, and people came and went asking him questions.

I approached. "Good morning."

He gave me a nod. "Hello."

"I'm Sophie Crush."

"Michael Hume."

"Nice to meet you, Michael."

"Line that one up with the pillar. Six foot spacing," he called out to a pair of workers who were placing a table. To me, he asked, "Can I help you with something?" He didn't seem annoyed, just busy and distracted.

I got that. "Do you have a solid attendance estimate?"

He seemed surprised by the question. "Two hundred twenty-five."

I did a quick scan of the space. "Buffet or table service?"

Now he was looking a little less patient. "Buffet. And you are?"

"The person in charge," Stone announced from behind me.

I hadn't heard him approach.

Michael saw Stone and his impatience vanished.

"I'm not trying to take over," I said to Stone. I wasn't sure why he'd spoken so firmly.

"I'm deputizing you," he said. "Sophie can take over the dining plans."

"Of course," Michael said to Stone. "I didn't realize."

"Neither did I," I said, trying to make light. I didn't want to get off on the wrong foot with Michael. I just had a few suggestions.

"She knows what she's doing," Stone said. "She used to run a restaurant in Seattle."

Stone was overstating. I hadn't been in charge of the entire Blue Fern restaurant, just the dining room service.

"What did you want to change?" he asked me.

I decided to plunge in. Hoping that Michael wouldn't react too badly to my ideas. "I was thinking round tables would work better than rectangular."

"Rectangular was the order," Michael said in a cautionary tone. "It's been the tradition for years."

"Do you have rounds available?" I asked.

"Yes, but—"

"Let's exchange them," Stone said.

"It'll take extra time."

"Is it reasonable?" I asked. "Costly?" I could picture the setup in my mind, and I liked the way it looked. I also knew the conversational flow of rounds was much superior to rectangles. But I didn't want to be obstinate about it.

"There'd be some overtime tonight," Michael said.

"Not a problem," Stone said. "We want it to be the best."

"Rounds would be best," I said.

"Done," Stone said.

Michael clamped his jaw but kept his tone on a professional level. "Rounds it is." He gave a whistle.

Everyone who was working looked up, and he paced toward them.

"I hope I didn't cause him too much grief," I said.

Stone shrugged. "We're paying him to get it right. And I trust your ideas. Anything else?"

"Did you ever consider table service instead of buffet?"

I could tell by his expression that he had not. "Talk to the caterer. It's Mel and Off-the-Land."

"*Me* talk to them?"

"We've never had a restaurant professional in the company before."

"I'm not in the company," I said.

"You know what I mean."

As two men passed by us removing the big tables, Stone canted his head toward the entrance. "Come on. I'll take you to see her."

I followed along. "Who?"

"Mel."

"Mel's a woman?"

"She is. You'll like her."

"Can you just do this?" I asked, glancing around behind us at the organized chaos.

"Mel won't mind the interruption. We're one of her biggest events of the year."

We were heading up the back driveway in the general direction of the garage.

"I mean use my ideas to change the party."

"You volunteered."

"All I said was round tables."

"And table service. It's all on you now, Sophie."

"Ha, ha."

We approached a pickup truck and Stone opened the passenger door. "You seem to like this kind of thing."

He was right. I did like this kind of thing. There was a reason I'd gone into dining room management. I got a kick out of planning dining experiences and an immense level of satisfaction out of seeing people have a good time.

"Hop in," he said.

"I thought we were going to see Mel?" I looked around for a car or van marked Off-the-Land.

"We are."

"She's not here?"

"She'll be at her restaurant in town."

I met his gaze. We were a couple of feet apart, but I could still feel his magnetism. I hadn't been thinking about it during our exchange, but for some reason it hit me all at once.

"You're going to drop everything and drive me into Anchorage."

The timbre of his voice was deep. "I am."

"Why?"

His gaze bored into mine, reigniting all the feelings I'd been struggling to keep at bay. "I think you know why."

"I don't." I dared to hope he'd say something flattering or complimentary, that he liked me or wanted to spend time with me or something like that. I wished I didn't feel that way, but I did.

"For Braxton," he said. "He'll like it that you're getting involved in the event."

Disappointment hit me before I could stop myself.

This was for Braxton, not Stone.

Five

I'd driven into Anchorage a few times now, and the trip down the highway that had seemed so long on that first drive from the airport felt shorter. At least it had on my last trip. Not so much this time, since I was stuck in the cab alone with Stone.

I knew he couldn't read my mind. He didn't know that I'd been deflated like a teenager with a crush back there. But I knew, and I really wanted this trip to be over.

Instead, the miles churned slowly past as we drove the winding road that followed the water's edge.

Something black flashed in my vision.

"Whoa," Stone said, cranking the wheel.

I was thrown his way. My seat belt snapped tight as I grasped for the armrest.

My brain sorted out the image, and I realized it was a bear. No, two bears. No, three—a mother and two cubs.

"Look out," I said reflexively, even though he could

see everything I could see and was taking every possible evasive maneuver.

The ditch was deep on my side of the pickup, the rock face beyond it steep and immovable. There was a cliff on the other side down to the water, and I sure didn't want to go over that. I didn't know what we were going to hit, but we were going to hit something—if not the bears, then the mountainside.

But suddenly the truck righted. It rocked on its wheels, gravel spun from beneath us, and in an instant we were headed up a narrow side road cut into the hill.

"You okay?" Stone asked, slowing the vehicle.

I gave a jerky nod. "Fine. Startled. That was a bear." I craned my neck to look out the back window, but we'd gone around a curve on the narrow road and I couldn't see the highway any longer.

"That was a bear," Stone confirmed, bringing us to a full stop. He put the shifter into Park. "You're not hurt? Did you wrench your neck?" He looked me over closely.

I stretched my neck back and forth, checking for pain or stiffness. "All good, I think. Does that happen a lot?"

"Occasionally. Usually it's moose that startle and run out in front of you. Bears seem to have more traffic sense."

"Good to know."

Stone gave a grin, a handsome, blue-eyes-lighting grin that, despite the situation, wormed its way to my toes. Why did he have to be so attractive?

"They can both wreck your car, flip it even and cause fatalities."

"I plan to be careful." I did—very careful driving from here on in.

Stone's reactions were faster than mine would have been.

"Good thing this road was here." If he hadn't taken the hidden turn, we'd have crashed.

"It leads up to Horn Lake," he said, nodding forward. "Really pretty green from the glacial runoff. You can ride horses up the back trail to get to it. We swam in it once when we were teenagers. Nearly killed us. But we were dumb back then."

"You, Mason and Kyle?"

"We pilfered a bottle from the whiskey cellar and drank it first."

"I guess you'd have to."

"Found out later it was a *very* expensive bottle, but that's another story. That night we dared each other to duck under the water. Once one of us took up the challenge, the rest had to put up or shut up."

"Who took up the challenge?"

His expression told me it was him.

"You had something to prove?" I guessed.

"Let's say I didn't have the genteel upbringing of Mason and Kyle. In my formative years, if someone dared you, you did it. It was the only way to keep their respect and keep yourself safe."

"That's sad." I couldn't help but feel sorry about his rough childhood.

"It's not sad. Mostly it was exhilarating. Plus, it worked. When I was younger, the other guys left me alone." He gave a chuckle. "That time it was worth it to see the expressions on Mason's and Kyle's faces."

"Exactly how cold was the lake?"

"Only a little above freezing. You can see the glacier where it runs off."

"Yeah?" I found myself looking up the road, curious about the site of Stone's youthful hijinks.

"You want to go see?" he asked.

My curiosity must have been obvious. "Would it take long?"

He pulled the transfer case into four-wheel drive. "It's a few miles."

"Do we have time?" I'd already interrupted his day.

"Sure." He pulled slowly ahead.

As we trundled along the narrow, rutted road, I found myself excited at the prospect of seeing Horn Lake and the glacier. First, it sounded beautiful. Second, I wanted to picture Stone, Mason and Kyle in their teenage years, having fun.

I'd attended parties and pulled a few silly stunts when I was in high school, but I had a feeling my antics were small-time compared to Stone and my newfound cousins.

The road became steeper, and Stone was forced to negotiate around big boulders. Trees crowded in around us as the truck rocked back and forth, tossing me around.

"Hang on," Stone said, indicating the top corner on my side as he wrestled with the steering wheel.

I looked up to see a handhold, and I grabbed it. "Thanks. Are you sure we can make it?"

He gave me a fleeting look of surprise. "It's easier on horses, but we'll get there."

"It's so rough." I'd never been on a road remotely like this before.

"This is nothing," he said. "You're not getting motion sickness are you?"

"No. I'm fine."

"Good. Just a couple more miles."

"A couple more *miles*?" I'd been expecting the lake to appear at any moment.

He flashed an unabashed grin. "We picked it because it was private."

"For your stolen moments of drinking."

"And swearing like lumberjacks, and a little making out on occasion."

I felt myself go hot at the image of Stone making out. I looked away before he could see a blush come up on my face. The last thing I wanted was for him to know I'd put myself in that particular image with him.

"Does it get worse?" I asked to change the subject.

"The road?"

"Yes."

"A little bit, right near the top. You kind of have to take a run at the last bit."

"Oh, good."

"It's fun."

"I can't wait," I said sarcastically, wondering what I'd gotten myself into.

We bumped our way around a few more bends, and then he pressed the accelerator. "Hang on."

I gripped the handle and reached out to grasp the back of the bench seat.

The truck went faster, rattling the frame, rattling my teeth. Then an impossibly steep embankment loomed up in front of us.

"We're going up *that*?" I asked as the truck shifted gears.

"I've done it dozens of times," Stone said. He was hanging tight to the steering wheel, his shoulders stiff and his back planted hard against the cushioned seat.

I closed my eyes, felt the cab tip up in front, heard the wheels spin in the dirt, then for a second it felt like we were floating.

We came down hard, and I felt the shock up my spine.

"See?" Stone said as everything slowly stilled. "Wasn't that fun?"

My first glimpse of Horn Lake confirmed it was spectacular. Crystal clear turquoise water surrounded by lush forest, with a gleaming white glacier in the distance against a stark blue sky.

Stone spun the truck in a tight circle, so we were facing the road. His arms stretched across the back of the seat as he looked over his shoulder going in Reverse. He rocked us to a stop, put the truck into Park and set the brake. "Come and take a look."

He unfastened his seat belt, and I did the same, opening my door to slide from the high seat onto the dirt. Then I shaded my eyes to gaze at the view as we walked to the back of the truck.

He dropped the tailgate, giving us a high seat. "Boost up?"

"In a minute." First, I wanted to check the temperature of the water.

I crouched down to where miniwaves lapped the pebbled shore and dipped my fingers into the water. It was painfully cold.

"Ouch," I said, immediately pulling my hand back.

"Cold, huh?" he asked, stopping next to me.

I rose. "Freezing."

"Yeah, we were pretty wild back then. I don't know how long it takes to get to hypothermia in that temperature, but it can't be long."

"Are you saying you were lucky to live through your youth?"

"Now you see what Braxton had to work with."

I had thought about that a few times, wondering what kind of a man would take in a rebellious teenager who'd vandalized his property. It was admirable. There were obviously things about Braxton I didn't yet understand.

From a genetic perspective, it was encouraging. I might have inherited some of his short temper, but maybe I'd also inherited some of his hidden benevolence.

"Do you know why he did it?" I asked.

Stone shrugged. "It's still a mystery to me. I sure didn't deserve it."

"You're selling yourself short."

"I'm not. I was a little jerk back then. It took a long time for me to appreciate what he did for me. It took— Will you look at that." Stone pointed to the sky.

I followed his gesture to see a pair of huge birds floating in the sky.

"Golden eagles," he said. "That'll be a mating pair. They likely have a nest nearby."

I'd seen bald eagles from the house, but this was the first time I'd seen goldens. I watched them soar in silent circles above us, their wingspan impressively broad and silhouetted against the sky.

I moved my gaze back to earth and had to blink to adjust my vision from the brightness. "What were you saying?"

He crouched and splashed his hand in the water. "Are you up for a swim?"

"No way."

"You're sure? Ah, that's what I remember. Refreshing."

"About Braxton…" I tried to coax him, being curious about the relationship of the two men.

"What about Braxton?"

"You were saying something."

Stone picked up a handful of rocks and tossed one into the lake. "Only that it was tough at first. I went from an overcrowded three-bedroom foster home to…well, you've seen it."

"The Cambridge mansion."

He tossed another rock that made a long arc before splashing into the smooth water. "They gave me a bedroom bigger than my old backyard."

"Funny," I said, thinking about my own change in circumstance. I was an adult and had made my own decisions to get here. But both our experiences had been sudden and dramatic.

"Funny?" he prompted.

"My newfound wealth is a culture shock. I'm not saying it's the same thing as you went through. But my friend Tasha had to drag me out house shopping. I wanted something on the water. I love the idea of being on the oceanfront. But the houses there, they were all so big. Not mansion big, but too big for one person."

"You said you just bought a new house."

"I did."

"So, you found one you liked."

"With five bedrooms. What am I going to do with five bedrooms?"

"You'll figure it out." He threw the last rock, then dusted off his hands.

"That's what Tasha said."

"She sounds very smart." He gestured to the tailgate, and we made our way back. There, he gave me a quick boost, just a couple of seconds, but the ghost of his touch lingered at my hips.

"She is very smart," I said to distract myself. "She completely revamped her life, got married and joined the library board. She does a reading outreach program for kids."

He sat next to me. "Good for her."

I took in the sweep of the view, thinking about Tasha and Layla and Brooklyn. "All my friends seem happy being rich."

"You have nothing but rich friends?"

I didn't want him to get the wrong idea. "They didn't used to be rich. Believe me, we were all perfectly average. It happened sort of unexpectedly for each of them.

You know, maybe it was easier with husbands. They didn't have to do it alone."

I pondered the theory for a moment. It might be easier with a partner. It made sense. You could talk things out, exchange ideas, get past the strangeness of it all together.

"Layla and Brooklyn married into money," I continued. "Twin brothers."

"Yeah?"

"Max and Colton were already rich, so they obviously knew what they were doing." Something big and black registered in my peripheral vision.

"They were also insulated from—"

The black thing suddenly moved, and I grabbed Stone's arm. "What's *that*?"

He took in my expression then jerked his head around. He immediately hopped to his feet in the truck box and pulled me up with him. "That's our bear."

I moved closer, sticking tight to Stone. Every sense came alert and I could hear my heart pounding in my ears. "What does it want?" My voice was a rasp.

"She's curious."

The cubs were moving around their mother. One of them came up on its hind feet and sniffed the air.

"Are they hungry?" I didn't really want an answer to that.

"Bears don't eat people." Stone paused. "Mostly anyway."

"Mostly," I squeaked in a whisper.

One of the cubs gave a cry.

The mother huffed and came up on her hind legs.

My eyes went wide. She was *huge*.

"Back up to the cab." He urged me that way. "Nice and slow, nothing sudden."

"Can she get us up here?" I asked, knowing it was a stupid question. The bear could probably hop into the truck box without breaking her stride.

As we backed into the cab, her ears went back and she huffed again. The two cubs rushed to hide behind her, and I couldn't help thinking that was a bad sign.

"I'm going to jump out on the driver's side," Stone said in an undertone.

"You're *leaving* me?"

"Can you follow?"

"Yes." I nodded rapidly. I'd follow him anywhere in a situation like this.

"I'll open the door, and I want you to dive inside as fast as you can. I'll be right behind you."

"Right. Got it."

The bear dropped back down to all fours and gave a deafening roar.

"Now," Stone said and put his hand on the side of the box, hopping over and grabbing the door handle.

I clambered over much less gracefully, scratching my belly and tearing my shirt. But I hit the ground feetfirst and lunged for the door, scrambling inside, aware of the bear charging around the back of the truck. Her feet pounded on the ground, sending out sharp vibrations.

Stone's hand pushed against my butt, shoving me unceremoniously forward. Then I heard the door slam behind him.

I dared to look and saw the bear rear up, her big paws going on the roof as she roared against the glass.

"Can she get in?" I managed to ask.

Stone started the engine. "We're not sticking around to find out."

The noise had seemed to surprise the bear, and it dropped away, giving Stone a chance to lurch forward. We bounced crazily down the incline.

I hadn't had time to put on my seat belt, and I fell off the seat, my knee hitting the floor.

"You okay?" Stone called.

"Good," I said. "Fine. Keep going."

He glanced in the mirror. "She's not following."

The ride got a bit smoother as Stone slowed us down.

"Can you get up?" he asked.

"Yeah. Sure." I shakily pulled myself up on the seat and reached for my seat belt, clicking it securely into place.

Stone pulled his own across his chest with one hand. "Can you help me with mine?"

I reached over. Our hands mingled above the mechanism, getting it sorted out in the right direction, then I clicked the seat belt in.

I rose and sat back, blowing out a breath. "Has that ever happened before?"

"Not here," he said. "Grizzly encounters are unusual."

"So, that was special?" I managed a shaky laugh.

"Very special." He glanced my way. "Seriously. Are you okay? Your adrenaline's still pumping, so you might not feel it yet."

He was right about that.

"I banged my knee, but it's just a bruise."

"Your shirt's ripped."

I pulled back the torn bit to look. "Just a scratch."

"You're bleeding."

"Barely." It was starting to sting now, but it wasn't a deep cut. I dabbed at it with the end of my shirt. "You?" I asked. "Any injuries?"

"None. Good cardio workout there for a minute." He laughed too. His sounded a lot less flustered than me.

We drove a few minutes more in silence.

"Thanks," I finally remembered to say.

He glanced at me again, his brow going up. "For putting you in danger?"

"For staying so calm, for knowing what to do."

"I'd never have left you in the box, you know."

"I know." I did know. I knew that now more than ever. I realized my hair was a mess, hanging over my eyes. When I smoothed it back, I saw my hand was shaking. It was the adrenaline coming out of my system.

"Hey," Stone said, his voice laced with concern.

Before I knew it, he'd stopped the truck, released our seat belts and drawn me into his arms. He felt solid, strong, incredibly reassuring, even though I knew we were out of danger now.

"You're fine," he said soothingly against my hair.

I nodded in response. "I know. It's just the adrenaline."

"Adrenaline is good."

"Especially around bears."

He chuckled. "Good for you, Sophie."

"Good for me what?"

"Bouncing back, making a joke, not turning all anxious."

It hadn't even occurred to me to get anxious. Not that there'd been time. Stone's reactions had been fast, smart and decisive.

"Thanks, Stone," I whispered again. I put my arms around him, hugging him tight in gratitude.

We silently held each other for a long minute, then his lips brushed my temple with the lightest of kisses. My chest went tight. My skin heated in reaction. My limbs tingled and I unconsciously arched my body against him.

He kissed me again, more firmly this time, making his way along my cheek, down and down. Then he pulled back a little. His palm cupped the back of my neck. He gazed into my eyes, his own full of questions.

I nodded in answer, and he tipped forward, kissing me full on the lips.

Joy rushed through me. I was thrilled to be alive, thrilled to be in Stone's arms. The wilderness around us was vast and energizing, and for the first time I didn't feel so much like a spectator in Alaska. I had a toehold on belonging.

Our lips fused, the kiss going deeper. Desire and arousal rushed through me. His shirt was thin cotton, and I could feel the heat of his chest seeping into my breasts.

He bracketed my hips, tugging me along the bench seat, easing me back until he was lying on top of me. His lips left mine, moving to my neck, planting hot, sexy kisses along the tender skin.

I shivered in reaction as his lips left imprints of arousal in a chain toward my chest. He popped the buttons on my shirt, and I held my breath, waiting for his touch on my breasts. My bra was thin silk, and I could feel my nipples tightening against the fabric, waiting more desperately for his touch as the seconds ticked past.

Then his mouth touched me, dampening the silk fabric, drawing the hard nub into the cavern of his mouth. It was the sexiest sensation I'd ever felt, and I gasped, arching, looking for more. He obliged, moving to the other breast.

I tugged at his shirt, dragging it over his head. I wanted to feel skin on skin, our bodies together. He ducked his way free and tossed the shirt aside. He pushed my shirt off my shoulders, trapping my arms with the final buttons.

He looked deep into my eyes, then teased my breasts again as he freed the last of my buttons. I all but tore off my shirt and impatiently ripped my bra over my head. Then I dived headlong in, pressing my breasts against his skin, wrapping my arms around his neck, kissing him deeply, letting my imagination run wild to making love, our bodies together, completing each other.

"Sophie." His voice sounded a long way away.

"Yes," I said. "Oh, yes." I reached for the snap on his jeans.

"Sophie," he said again.

"Stone," I said back. *Stone, Stone, Stone*, my mind echoed.

His hand covered mine, stopping my quest to release his zipper.

I looked up, more than a little puzzled.

His expression was tight, his lips drawn thin. His voice was a rasp when he spoke. "I wasn't thinking of this."

My brain was a muddle of confusion.

"We…" He scrunched his eyes shut.

He was saying no? He was saying *no*? We were one step away from paradise here. I didn't know about him, but passion like this didn't come along every day in my world.

"Are you okay?" I asked, stupefied. I might not be the most experienced woman in the world, nor a genius, but I could tell when a guy was into me, and Stone was very, very much into me right now.

He pushed my hand from his fly. "Not a good idea."

"No," I said. "It's a *great* idea."

"Sophie," he said, and his forehead dropped lightly against mine. He held it there.

"What?" I asked.

"We're reacting to the scare. It's a hormone thing."

I could agree it was hormones, but I wasn't agreeing with the rest. "We kissed long before that bear came along."

"We didn't do *this*," he said, drawing back to look. His gaze dropped to my bare breasts and stayed there.

"We wanted to," I said. At least I'd wanted to, and it sure seemed like Stone did too, even back then.

He picked my shirt up from the floor and pushed it against me, covering my breasts. "This is way too complicated."

The passion was rapidly disappearing out of me now. A woman could only stay hot for a guy so long while he was rejecting her. I shook out my shirt.

Stone looked pointedly away as I pushed my arms into my sleeves and did up the buttons. My bra dangled from the seat beside me, and I stuffed it into my jeans pocket. Then I smoothed out my shirt.

"There," I said, an edge to my voice. "Happy?"

He looked at me like I'd lost the plot. "No. Ticked off."

He was mad at me? Come on.

I turned in my seat, facing forward, tipping my chin, my body language telling him I was ready to go now. "You're the one who called a halt."

He drew back. "Not at *you*. At myself. At the circumstances." He moved back to the driver's seat, grasping the steering wheel. "You don't know who I am, Sophie."

"Yeah, well, you don't know who I am either. Is that a prerequisite to sex?"

"Yes."

I turned to give him a look of disbelief. *"Really?"*

His expression turned sheepish. "Not always. But in this case, yes. Yes, it is."

"Why?" I was genuinely curious. Our situation was complicated, sure. But we were both adults. We were entitled to make up our own minds about how we felt about each other. It was nobody else's business.

"You're his daughter."

"This is about *Braxton*?" A man I barely even knew was messing with my sex life?

"Yes."

I gave my head a little shake. "You won't touch me because of some warped sense of loyalty to him?"

"I touched you plenty."

"You do know I make my own decisions, right?"

Stone's knuckles went white as he gripped harder on the steering wheel. "That's irrelevant."

"I'm an adult, Stone. My personal life is none of Braxton Cambridge's business."

"That's my point. We're not going to tell him."

The statement took me by surprise. "Of course, we're not going to tell him. Why on earth would we tell him?"

"Exactly. And then I'd have a secret...from him. That's not the way I operate." He pulled his seat belt around himself. "Buckle up."

"Are you saying this conversation's over?"

"Yes."

I stared at his profile a moment longer. I wanted him, and he wanted me. I didn't see where Braxton had anything at all to do with it. But I sure wasn't going to beg.

"Sophie."

"Fine." I jerked hard and reeled the seat belt out. "Have it your way."

I was surprised when Stone turned toward Anchorage instead of back to the Cambridge mansion. I had no idea why he'd want to stay trapped with me any longer than absolutely necessary.

"We're still going to Off-the-Land?" I asked.

He brought up the truck's speed. "That was the whole point of the trip."

That had been the original point, but things had gone significantly off the rails since then.

"Nothing's changed," he said.

I felt like quite a lot had changed. "That's your perspective?"

"It's a fact not a perspective. You're going to meet Mel, talk about ideas for the party, share your expertise, get yourself involved in the event and the family. Everybody wins."

I didn't feel like pussyfooting around. "This doesn't make you uncomfortable?"

"That I stuck with my principles? No, that never makes me uncomfortable."

"Well, I'm uncomfortable." I didn't like sitting here with a guy who'd just turned me down for a reason he had yet to explain.

"Get over it."

"That's your whole answer, *get over it*?"

"As you so aptly pointed out earlier, we're both adults. There's some sexual chemistry between us, sure, but we can handle it. We can make a choice whether or not to act on it."

That wasn't the entire point. But I was sure I wouldn't be acting on it again anytime soon. If that's how he wanted to play it…

"Fine." My tone was clipped.

"Good." He responded in kind.

"Tell me something about Mel." Now that it was settled, I was anxious to move on.

"Sure."

We took a turn at speed and I hung on to the handle to keep from swinging his way. The tires didn't break loose beneath us, so I assumed he knew what he was doing.

"Mel's great," he said, his tone returning to normal. "Smart, down-to-earth. She inherited the business from her dad, who inherited it from his dad. Off-the-Land has been in operation since the gold rush."

I couldn't help but be intrigued. That was a very long time to be in business. "Is it catering only, or do they have a dining room?"

"I guess you could call it a dining room. They have a seating area. It's casual. Their clientele tends to be working-class guys looking for a hot, filling lunch to either take out or eat in."

"I see." I'd expected the barbecue to be more high-end than this was sounding.

"What do you see?" Stone asked.

"Off-the-Land doesn't sound like what I was expecting."

"Which was?"

"Something a little more…"

"Posh?"

"Not posh." I reframed my expectations. "I guess it *is* a barbecue."

"Are you a snob, Sophie Crush?" His teasing tone surprised me.

I'd expected us to stay aloof with each other for a whole lot longer than this. "I'm not a snob. But the Cambridges have gone to a lot of trouble for this—the tent, the temporary dance floor, grooming the yard. It has to be costing a fortune."

"It's our way of thanking the employees. We're not going to skimp."

"So why the lowbrow caterer?"

"Did I say *lowbrow*?" He wasn't teasing any longer.

"No. But you made it sound as if—"

"Mel's cooking is amazing. I hope you're not going to act like this when we get there."

Now I was insulted. "Act like what? I'll be perfectly polite."

"And respectful."

"*Yes*, respectful. What do you think of me, Stone?"

He did a sweeping look at me as we drove past the first buildings in town. "That you're big-city."

"Seattle?" We were pretty laid-back in Seattle compared to, well, pretty much any other big city in the entire county.

"This is Alaska. We're grounded and hardworking. We take things at face value."

"Fine," I said. Then my tone turned sarcastic. "I'll be on my best behavior."

"Just don't have any preconceived ideas, is all."

"I don't have any preconceived—"

He shot me a look.

"You said it was rustic," I reminded him.

"Rustic can be good."

I was tired of arguing. "Fine. Sure. Rustic can be great."

"Say it with a little more enthusiasm." He was teasing again. It was hard to keep up with the man's mood swings.

"Rustic can be great," I said with sincerity. It helped that I believed it was true.

"That's the spirit." He flipped on his signal then and swung the truck into a big gravel-strewn parking lot.

A sign above the sprawling plain brown building read: Off-the-Land Restaurant and Catering, Est. 1898. The building didn't look like it had been around since 1898, but it did look like it had probably been in place since the fifties.

Stone parked the truck out front, and we both exited into a slightly dusty breeze.

We crossed a creaky porch and he pulled on a large raw wood handle. The door screeched open on rusty hinges, and he motioned me in.

The restaurant was dim inside; a few narrow windows let in some murky daylight. A dozen picnic-style tables were set out in two rows with a scarred bar stretching behind them. Two glass-fronted drink coolers stood behind

BARBARA DUNLOP   107

the bar, bathing the area in fluorescent light. I could just make out a row of plain wooden bar stools pushed underneath.

There were no tablecloths, but each table had a tin coffeepot stuffed with paper napkins next to a mismatched pair of salt and pepper shakers, a ketchup dispenser and a bottle of Tabasco sauce. I reminded myself of all the things Stone had said. It wasn't for me to be judgmental.

"Well, hello there, Stone!" A woman burst through a set of swinging half doors from the kitchen. She was tall, probably close to six feet. She had flaming red hair twirled up in a bun, an attractive face and a pair of gold-rimmed glasses perched on her straight nose.

"Hey, Mel," Stone replied.

Mel's curious expression turned my way.

"This is Sophie Crush. She's up from Seattle and helping with the barbecue."

"Nice to meet you, Sophie," Mel said, coming closer.

"Sophie used to be in the restaurant business."

Mel's expression faltered for a second. "You bringing in the big guns?" she asked Stone.

"Nothing like that," Stone quickly said.

"I'm just a friend," I added. "Visiting. I was watching them set up in the Cambridges' yard and got curious."

"Oh. What can I do for your curiosity?"

I hoped we hadn't got off on the wrong foot already. "I'd love to hear the menu."

Mel perked up. "Sure. Come on inside and take a look."

Slightly bemused, I followed her back through the swinging doors and into the industrial kitchen.

Stone brought up the rear.

Unlike the front of the restaurant, the kitchen was bright, modern and stocked with up-to-date stainless steel equipment. It was easy to see that half of it was devoted to meal preparation and the other half was set up as a bakery.

Three men were working on the kitchen side, two at a salad counter and one over the grill. Farther in the bakery, a woman removed a tray of tarts from the oven. They smelled delicious.

"You do your own baking?" I asked. It wasn't unheard of to combine both businesses, but it was unusual. Back at The Blue Fern we'd taken a daily order from a nearby bakery. They had their specialty, and we had ours.

"It's a significant part of our business," she said. "We go through sourdough like nobody's business."

"Bread?" I asked.

"And our hamburger buns." She gestured to a multi-tiered cooling rack. "Most of the baking goes out in the morning, but burgers are on the dinner menu and grilled sandwiches too. We serve them with soup at lunchtime. Fries are more popular for the dinner crowd, and the chili, my secret recipe. It travels really well for takeout."

"This is an impressive setup." I looked all around.

"For the Kodiak Communications barbecue, we'll have burgers, of course. But chicken burgers too."

"Breaded?" I asked, picturing fast-food chicken burgers.

"Grilled. They were popular last year, and a couple of people asked about adding pesto to the condiments. I think it's a good idea."

"I love that idea," I said. "Have you considered offering avocado?" It was another fresh taste that could liven up a traditional menu.

"I hadn't… But, you know, we could do a Tex-Mex version with guacamole and salsa."

"What about the classic T-bones?" Stone asked. "Baked potato, sourdough rolls, coleslaw."

"You're unimaginative," I said.

"We'll have all that, Stone," Mel said with a laugh. "Don't you worry."

"Another word for *unimaginative* is *hungry*," Stone said. "A slice of avocado's not going to do it for me."

"Don't forget about dessert," Mel said, giving him a playful tap on the arm. "Bumbleberry pie and chocolate layer cake."

"Some of your ice cream," Stone asked hopefully.

I couldn't help but think Stone and I would get along just fine on the dessert front.

"Mason put in a request for mint chocolate. We'll do a batch of vanilla as usual. It'll go with anything."

"You make your own ice cream?" I asked.

"Jack-of-all-trades," Mel said.

"I'd say master-of-all-trades," Stone said.

The baker slid a tray of tarts into the cooling rack below the sourdough buns.

"Are those the bumbleberry?" I couldn't help asking.

"Try one?" Mel asked.

"I sure will." Stone moved as she spoke, beelining for the cooling rack.

I couldn't help but smile at his enthusiasm.

"I'll get you a plate," Mel said to me.

"Got any ice cream?" Stone asked.

"You're shameless," I told him.

"She's used to me."

"I am that," Mel said. "You should have seen him as a teenager, a bottomless pit."

"I burned a lot of calories while I was growing."

"I hope he ate more than just tarts." I had to admit to feeling a little jealous at the thought of being able to indulge in all the desserts I wanted without fear of gaining an ounce.

"Her cake's good too," Stone said with a smirk.

Mel handed each of us a plate and a little fork. "Help yourselves. I'll get the ice cream."

"You have to try them with the ice cream," Stone said to me. "Especially when they're hot like this. You haven't truly lived until you've tasted one of Mel's tarts à la mode."

Mel laughed and bustled off to a walk-in freezer.

"I told you you'd like her," Stone said in an undertone, even as he transferred two tarts to his plate.

"I do like her." I settled for a single tart. A corner of the pastry flaked off on my plate, and the rich aroma filled my nostrils, rousing my salivary glands.

"All I've got is vanilla," Mel called out as she returned to us with a tub of ice cream in her hand. She set it down on the wide stainless steel counter, peeled off the lid and pulled open a drawer to extract a scoop.

"Sophie?" she asked, scoop at the ready.

"Absolutely," I said, feeling privileged at the chance to try such a delicacy.

She popped a scoop of the vanilla-bean-speckled ice cream next to my tart. Then she nodded across the wide aisle to a rolling stool. "Grab a seat."

Stone set his tart plate on the counter and retrieved three stools for us to sit down while Mel gave him a double scoop of the ice cream.

"Not joining us?" he asked her as she covered the tub up.

"I have to pace myself," she said. Her eyes twinkled in my direction. "I can't wait to see what you think."

I cut into the pastry and the deep purple berry mixture ran free. I combined the bite with the ice cream and took my first taste. The flavors all but burst in my mouth—tart berries with tender pastry and sweet cold vanilla. "Oh, my." I touched my lips with two fingers.

Stone took a big bite too and grinned at me.

"This is awesome," I told Mel. I was impressed with her skill. And for a moment I felt guilty about the money I was making from Sweet Tech. Our technology might turn out beautiful creations, but they couldn't compete with Mel's for flavor.

Her grin went wide. "Thanks."

"Truly awesome."

What was she doing hiding up here in Alaska? With a talent like hers, she could be making a fortune anywhere in the country.

"Did I steer you right, or what?" Stone asked me.

"My faith in you is renewed." A whole different kind of warmth rushed through me as our gazes met and held.

Six

The backyard could only be described as organized chaos. Mel had said she'd consider table service if I would be willing to put together a selection of six plated meals. She'd also need another kitchen tent connected to the dining tent where the additional staff could work.

Stone had shrugged off the cost, and I'd decided he had mastered being rich. The extra tent was going up now, and Adeline was sitting next to me on the deck watching the progress.

She was curled up in a deep cushioned all-weather chair, while I had my laptop balanced on my knees, not really thrilled about either potato salad or fries as an accompaniment to the chicken pesto burgers.

"Does Mel serve yam fries?" I asked Adeline.

"Not that I've seen."

"Do you think she might?" Yam fries would be a nice

differentiator between the fresher chicken burger and the more traditional beef burger.

"Probably," Adeline said. "Hey, what's that?"

I glanced at Adeline, then looked to where her attention was focused. A group of workers were hoisting a tall lighting scaffold up above the bandstand.

"That's impressive." Hoisting the thirty-foot scaffolding looked tricky.

"Isn't he though?" Adeline fanned her face with her hand. "They don't build them like that in California."

I took in the six men working and zeroed in on a buff, square-chinned, dark haired man with giant biceps straining under a red plaid shirt. I had to admit, he looked full-on Alaska. "I thought California was the bodybuilding mecca of the country," I teased.

"Those muscles are for show. These ones are the real deal." She was smiling warmly now.

"For show?" I'd never heard of such a thing.

"They build 'em for style, every exercise calibrated to bulk up and give definition."

"And that's a bad thing, why?" I couldn't help but think about Stone.

I'd seen him without his shirt, admittedly it was through the fog of passion. But I saw enough of his washboard abs and defined pecs to know he was in fantastic shape. And I doubted his exercise was calibrated to do anything cosmetic.

"Look at that strength and power," Adeline said with a lilt to her voice.

I glanced over to see the red-shirted man vault onto the stage in one smooth motion. I had to admit, his physique didn't seem designed for show. "I take it you don't have a boyfriend in Sacramento?"

"No boyfriend." She continued watching the man work as she talked. "Broke up with a guy a couple of weeks ago."

"Was it serious?" I wondered if that could be part of the reason she'd come home early.

"He thought so. I didn't."

"Oh. Then I guess that's not the worst breakup a person ever had."

"He works in the Governor's Office. I met him when he gave an undergraduate lecture, and I sat in. I have to say, he's very good at the front of a room."

"Less so up close and personal?" I asked.

She gave a noncommittal shrug. "Politicians aren't my thing."

"Is he going into politics?"

"He's the chief of staff. At that level, they all have aspirations of running for office."

I hadn't known that. But I'd never known anyone who worked in a political office either.

"Is that why you came home?" I asked her flat out.

"No." She gestured to the mayhem of trucks and cranes and tents and crew. "I came home for this."

"You like chaos?"

"I like excitement. The lead-up is as exciting as the party. You must like it too, otherwise why would you work in a busy restaurant on a Saturday night instead of taking a nice steady office job?"

"I guess I like a certain level of excitement. Maybe that's why I'm not so wild about being rich. It's quiet, way too quiet."

"What's too quiet?" Stone appeared next to me. He looked out at the activity in obvious confusion.

"Sophie's life," Adeline said.

"I don't mean right this minute," I said.

"Glad to hear it." He levered into the chair next to mine. "How are the plated meals coming?"

I looked reflexively down at my laptop to find the screen had shut down. "I'm getting there. The trick is to be exciting and not too exotic. They have to appeal to a wide range of people but still have enough flavor and uniqueness to not be boring."

"Hence the idea of a buffet."

"Buffets are long lineups, your tablemates coming and going, people all eating at different times, cluttering up the dining room." I shook my head as I spoke. "Sit-down is much better, especially when the point of the event is to get people together who have something in common but don't get to socialize with each other very often. Sharing a good meal is wonderful for that."

"She sells it well," Adeline said.

"She does." Braxton's voice joined the conversation, startling me.

We'd seen each other since our private talk a few days back. But we were always in a group, and I still felt nervous around him, jumpy really.

"I hear you're making changes to the barbecue," he said. It was clear he was addressing me.

"A few things," I said without turning. "I talked them over with Mel. She has the final say, of course."

"I think it's a good idea," Braxton said. His voice was easy as he took the chair next to Stone. "The event could use some freshening up. And you have as much right as the rest of us to—"

"I wasn't asserting a right." I didn't want him to think I was taking advantage of my genetic connection to the family.

"Sophie," he said in a gentle warning.

I didn't turn, but he waited until I finally gave in and looked past Stone.

"I'm glad you're interested," he said, his eyes soft.

"I don't want to overstep."

"You couldn't if you tried. You're one of us now."

"It's not like they won't push back," Adeline said.

Braxton's look turned sharp on his niece.

"Oh, don't pretend," she retorted, seemingly unaffected by his silent criticism. "If you do something they don't like," she said to me, "they push back hard. If you've got the green light here, go for it, enjoy it."

"You're not helping," Braxton said to Adeline.

"She is," I said, still looking at Adeline. "Thanks. I think I will enjoy this."

Braxton huffed out a breath and rocked back in his chair.

I got the feeling he was less than pleased that I'd sided with Adeline. But Adeline looked thrilled that I'd stuck with her.

Adeline looked like she was having fun at the party. So did Braxton for that matter. He was circulating through the backyard crowd, greeting people like he was best friends with them all, acknowledging their spouses and children and receiving warmth and appreciation in return.

The dinner had gone over well, the table service seeming popular among the guests, who were more dressed up than I'd expected. Luckily, Adeline and I had taken a shopping trip into Anchorage, where she'd encouraged me to buy a kicky little rust-and-black dress with long loose sleeves over a pair of leggings to protect against the bugs that came out when the wind died down. She'd wisely advised on low wedge heels since we'd be walking on the grass.

Everyone had migrated out of the dining tent, and the

band was setting up on the low stage. It was still strange to see the sun high in the sky at nine o'clock. Alaskan summers had to be experienced to be believed.

Stone came alongside me. "Well, that went well."

"Mel is a real pro."

She'd hired dozens of extra staff for the plating and serving, and they'd pulled it off with efficiency and aplomb. The plated meals were well received, with tons of compliments for the chicken pesto burgers garnished with avocado. The entire cooking and serving staff had received a thunderous round of applause, orchestrated by Braxton, at the end of the meal.

"He's very good at hosting," I said, nodding to Braxton.

"His staff loves him. He makes a point of getting to know everyone who comes on board with the company."

"That's more than two hundred people," I said, surprised but seeing the evidence with my own eyes.

"It's a point of pride for him."

"I wouldn't have expected it."

"That's because you met family Braxton. Not many people get to do that."

"Family Braxton?" I was intrigued.

"There's family Braxton and business Braxton. Business Braxton is even-keeled, professional and impeccable."

"Where family Braxton can be…irritable and cantankerous."

"I was going to say *exacting*."

I turned my head to give Stone a look. "You can't bring yourself to criticize him, can you?"

"I'm just being accurate."

"You're being kind."

"I'm a kind guy."

"Ha!"

"When have I not been kind?"

"The day I first walked through the door."

His expression faltered. "Well, you know, I thought—"

"That I was trying to con Braxton."

"It sure looked that way at the time. And I didn't know you."

"You know me now."

He grinned like he'd just won an argument. "And now I'm kind."

"Now you're impossible."

He looked me up and down. "You look great by the way."

The compliment warmed me far more than it should. "Adeline steered me to this. She's got a great eye."

"It looks good on you." His gaze went warm on me, and it brought to life a shimmer of desire in the pit of my stomach.

"I thought we weren't going to do that," I said, feeling self-conscious. I knew he couldn't read my mind, but I was worried that he might see the heat in my expression.

"Do what?"

I tipped my head to gaze accusingly at him. "Don't play dumb."

"I've been rethinking," he said, his smile decidedly flirtatious.

"Rethinking *what*?" I wanted to make sure I understood. I had no desire to play games.

"Telling Braxton about us."

I was stunned to silence for a second. "You want to tell Braxton you're going to have sex with me?"

Stone laughed.

I shriveled a little bit in embarrassment.

He seemed to notice my expression. "Sorry."

"You're not nice," I said.

"I meant tell Braxton I wanted to take you out on a date. The rest, well, I'm not about to make any assumptions."

It wasn't much of an assumption, since I'd thrown myself at him on the seat in his truck. Still, I was puzzled by his change of heart. "Why?"

"Why do I want to date you?"

"Why are you willing to tell Braxton about it?"

He sidled a little closer. "Mostly because that's the only way I get to take you out. I was thinking dinner, maybe a little dancing?"

I searched his expression. "Something's going on here."

"Enjoying the event?" Braxton asked.

I hadn't seen him arrive. I pulled back from Stone, realizing I'd been drawn closer and closer to him while we talked.

"Yes," I answered.

"Good. Good." His smile was wide and his voice hearty.

I couldn't help but think this was business Braxton.

"People enjoyed the new dinner format," Stone said.

"They did! Thanks for that, Sophie. It was a great addition. I know Mel really liked working with you."

Okay, this felt weird, like I was interacting with a fake Braxton.

The bandleader shouted a greeting into the microphone, welcoming the crowd and drawing everyone's attention.

"Ah, here we go," Braxton said, sounding pleased. "This is the best part of the event."

"Kodiak employees are a dancing crowd," Stone said.

I could see people surge toward the dance floor as the band started to play.

"Why are you standing here like a bump on a log?" Braxton asked Stone. He cocked his head my way. "Be a gentleman and ask Sophie to dance."

Stone didn't seem surprised by the suggestion. He also didn't miss a beat. He held his hand out to me. "Sophie?"

I did miss a beat. Was Braxton tossing the two of us

together? Or was this just business Braxton being a good barbecue host?

Stone raised his brow as he waited for my answer.

"Sure." I wasn't about to be rude. Plus, well, I really liked the idea of dancing with Stone.

When he wiggled his fingers to encourage me, I got a little hitch in my breath. I put my hand in his and waited for the inevitable rush of heat from his skin up my arm and through to my chest.

We started for the dance floor, leaving Braxton behind.

"What was that?" I asked as we wove a path through the crowd.

People smiled and nodded at Stone, some of them tossed a hello his way.

"I have no idea," he said to me as he acknowledged the greetings.

"Was that business Braxton doing his duty?" I asked.

"I expect it was. I don't know what else it would have been."

"Okay," I said, still feeling unsettled. But we'd made it to the edge of the dance floor, and Stone turned me into his arms.

We merged in seconds, our rhythms matching, our steps in sync. I hadn't expected Stone to be such a smooth dancer.

"You're good at this," I said, gazing up, liking the view of him this close.

He smiled. "Lessons in high school."

"There's a lot of dancing in Alaska?"

"It's very popular. We're a fun-loving people. And in-door activities are big in the winter."

"I guess you must get bored with all that snow."

"Not bored. The daylight hours are short, but people

cross-country ski, go snowmobiling, go ice fishing or just get out for a walk or a horseback ride."

"What about when it's cold?"

"If it's really cold, we stay inside. Hence, the dancing. But anywhere above zero, there's plenty to do without huddling in your house."

"It's the rain in Seattle that keeps us inside. We have umbrellas, but we mostly use them to get to the store or the gym. We like our parks when it's sunny, and the beach—beach volleyball is super popular."

"Do you get out on the water?"

"Not me personally. It's not like California, where the water's warm and you can surf the sandy beaches for months at a time."

The band wound the song down, and I paused, waiting to see if Stone would head off the dance floor.

He stilled but kept me in his arms.

I was content to stay.

"Sophie!" Adeline called from a few feet away.

The band struck up a slower song, and Stone moved us into the rhythm.

"Hi," I called back over my shoulder.

She gave me a delighted, knowing grin and waggled her brow at Stone, obviously remembering my admission of kissing him.

"What was that?" Stone asked.

"I don't know," I lied. "The Cambridges can be odd."

"You're a Cambridge."

"I'm not—" I stopped myself. I was a Cambridge. "Only by an accident of genetics."

"Only *completely* by genetics. You're as Cambridge as they come."

I fell silent as melancholy came over me. I softened

against Stone, leaning into his strength as I'd done a couple of times before.

"Hey," he said. "What's wrong?"

I tried to put it into words. "Things are moving so fast."

"Life has a way of doing that."

I remembered that he'd been through his own rocky times. "It's like the past is fading and I can't seem to catch it. I don't want to lose it."

"You'll never lose it, Sophie. Your mom's always going to be your mom. I know my mom's always going to be mine." There was a hitch in his voice.

"Your mom?" It was the first time he'd mentioned her.

"She died when I was six—heck of a thing to learn on the third day of first grade."

"I'm so sorry." I felt terrible for bemoaning the twists and turns in my life when Stone's had been so much worse, so much more profound.

"It was bad," he said. "But it was a long time ago. I know now it wasn't her fault. It wasn't anyone's fault."

I tightened my hold on him, feeling an urge to comfort the young boy he'd been back then.

"It gets better," he told me. But his arms tightened around me too.

"My problems are nothing compared to yours," I said, feeling guilty for complaining.

"You've been blindsided, and it's only been a few days. You're allowed to feel confused and upset and angry."

"I'm not angry." It was true. I was sad and disoriented, but I wasn't angry. "Well, maybe with the hospital." I paused. "Then again, if they'd got it right, I wouldn't have met my mom, wouldn't have grown up with her, would have…"

"Don't go back to feeling guilty again," Stone said, his deep voice soft. "Nobody's fault, remember?"

"I know." I nodded. Intellectually, I did know that. And I could tell my emotions were slowly catching up.

Adeline was alone in the kitchen making coffee when I came downstairs. It was coming up on ten o'clock in the morning, but we'd all danced and laughed the night away, indulging in wine from the Cambridge cellar. My head felt a little woolly this morning, and I was looking forward to a shot of caffeine.

"Espresso?" Adeline asked. She was dressed in a pair of bright plaid flannel pajama bottoms and a worn lime-green T-shirt. Her auburn hair was half in, half out of a messy ponytail. Even with her makeup smeared, she still looked beautiful.

I'd managed to hold off the coffee craving long enough to comb my hair and dress in a pair of yoga pants and a loose-knit oversize sweater.

"Something smoother," I said. "Mocha?"

"Coming up." She pulled a cup from the cupboard and pushed a series of buttons on the machine.

"You're a lifesaver," I said, pulling myself up on a bar chair and leaning my elbows on the island.

"That was a blast," she said.

"It was," I agreed. I couldn't remember a more fun party.

Aside from those who'd taken their kids home early, the Kodiak Communications staff had danced, drunk and laughed into the wee hours. It was the strangest sensation trudging into the mansion at that time of night with the sun barely dipping below the northern horizon.

While my mocha brewed, Adeline sat down across from me and sipped her espresso. There was a twinkle in her eyes, an expressive display of emotion on a morning like this, I thought.

"You danced a lot last night," she said, then waited.

"I did." I stood up and rounded the island to retrieve my mocha. I took a sip before walking back to the island. It was delicious. "Yum."

"You and Stone looked like a pretty good idea last night," she said as I took my seat.

I couldn't stop my own smile of remembrance. "It was fun."

"And…" She leaned forward. "And…"

"And, nothing. We danced. The night ended. Most of us came back inside as a group."

"And…" she said, canting her head to the side to watch me closely.

"And I went to bed." I'd been exhilarated but exhausted.

Adeline leaned closer still, a look of expectation on her face.

"Alone." I took another sip of the mocha, a bigger one since it had cooled a little.

Her expression fell and her shoulders drooped.

I couldn't help but chuckle at her disappointment. The laugh hurt my head.

"Good morning, good morning," Braxton's voice boomed.

"Ouch, Uncle," Adeline said, pressing her fingertips to her temples.

"Serves you right." Xavier Cambridge, Adeline's father followed his brother, Braxton, into the kitchen. I'd met Xavier in passing last night as the party was getting underway.

"Good morning, Sophie," he said to me now.

"Good morning."

"You look a sight better than Adeline."

I wasn't sure I felt that much better than Adeline, but I didn't need to tell him that. "It was a wonderful party. I had a really great time."

"I hear you were the brains behind the sit-down dinner."

"Mel did all the work." I didn't want to take credit. The initial idea might have been mine, but Mel had jumped in, and she'd been the one to pull it off.

"Mel's amazing." Xavier beat Braxton to the coffee machine.

"Is Stone up?" Braxton asked.

Adeline shot me a look that had me wishing I could kick her under the table.

"I haven't seen him yet," I said.

Adeline shook her head and, thankfully, neutralized her expression. "Me neither."

"I was thinking of sending him up to the Seafoam Glacier installation," Braxton said.

Xavier looked confused. "This week?"

"No harm in getting a head start," Braxton said.

"You ticked off at him for something?" Xavier asked.

I stilled, listening, worried I might have done something last night that had annoyed Braxton. Did he not like the idea of me and Stone?

"No," Braxton said as Xavier handed him a cup of coffee. "It's not like it's mid-January. It's nice up there."

"It doesn't have to be Stone. You could send an engineer."

"Sophie." Braxton looked my way.

"Yes?" I found myself nervous. I didn't know what was going on, but Xavier seemed puzzled. And I'd seen business Braxton in action last night, so I knew he could cover his emotions when he wanted.

"You haven't seen anything outside Anchorage yet."

"Nowhere except here," I said.

"Kodiak Island is absolutely gorgeous this time of year."

"What are we talking about?" Stone sauntered through the opening from the great room, looking like he'd had a fine night's sleep, not showing a single sign of a hangover. He slid me a smile before looking at Braxton. "Something happen on Kodiak Island?"

"Seafoam Resort wants an upgrade."

"Already?" Stone asked, taking over the coffee machine as Xavier finished.

"They've added ten new chalets," Braxton said.

Stone paused, taking a quick look over his shoulder at Braxton. "You're really keeping up-to-date with them."

"Jack Nice asked me about it last night. They're going to some tourism shows on the Eastern Seaboard next month, and they want to offer video streaming and conferencing at the resort. It's a must-have for corporate customers."

"You can never have too much bandwidth," Stone said. He lifted his full coffee cup and turned back to us, taking a deep drink.

I saw a bit of puffiness around his eyes and decided he hadn't made it through last night completely unscathed. Somehow that made me feel better, more like a part of the gang.

"Why don't you take a run over there and make some technical recommendations."

Stone paused, his cup near his mouth, looking puzzled. He sent another quick glance my way. He was clearly confused too. "You need *me* to go out there?"

"It'll show them our level of commitment."

"I think upgrading their infrastructure will show them our commitment."

"Take Sophie along," Braxton said. His voice was blasé. Maybe a bit too blasé? Then again, maybe I was imagining things.

But there was a pause before Stone answered. "Yeah?"

"She's barely seen anything of the state. You can give her a flight-seeing tour along the way."

"I'd come along," Adeline said brightly.

It was clear from Braxton's expression that her offer came as a surprise.

"The scenery is spectacular," she said to me, enthusiasm mounting in her voice. "Mountains and glaciers, usually lots of wildlife."

"It's settled then," Braxton said.

Stone looked thoughtful, dividing his attention between Adeline and Braxton.

"Sounds great," I said, since everyone seemed to be waiting for my response.

"Perfect," Adeline said as she hopped up from her seat. "We should go into town this morning," she said to me.

It was a quick change of topics, but that was okay by me. "What for?"

"To return your rental car. It's silly to keep it."

"We have plenty of company trucks," Xavier said. "You're welcome to borrow one anytime."

"Sophie doesn't need to drive a truck," Adeline said with a frown for her father. "We'll go to the dealer, find her a nice SUV."

"You want me to buy a car?" The idea seemed outlandish since I was only staying for a few more days.

"Kodiak will buy it," Adeline said brightly. "We can always use something new in the fleet. You just get to pick it out."

"I'm not going to—"

"That's a good idea," Braxton said in a thoughtful tone. "You need something to use while you're here."

I realized the Cambridges operated on a whole different wealth level than I did, but impulsively buying a new vehicle for someone who'd rarely even be here seemed preposterous even for the überrich.

I downed some more of my coffee to jump-start my brain.

"And you should pick out a new bedroom," Braxton said to me.

"Huh?"

"You're in the guest section of the house. You need to settle in somewhere more permanent."

"I'm a guest," I said. "And I'm heading home soon."

"You'll be back, won't you?" Xavier asked. "If nothing else, you and I have only just met." He looked around at the group. "We all want you to feel comfortable while you're here."

"I'm perfectly comfortable." I polished off the coffee but was still feeling woozy. I didn't want another one right away. For some reason I thought a stack of pancakes might help.

"We want to make it easy for you to visit as often as possible," Xavier said. "You shouldn't have to clear out your stuff every time you come and go."

It occurred to me then that I was taking up space that they might want for other guests. I didn't want to get in the way. "Whatever works best for you."

"Come on," Adeline said to me, moving toward the shortcut to the main staircase. "I'll show you what we've got."

I couldn't stop myself from taking one more look at Stone as I was leaving. His expression was still thoughtful, but it didn't give me a clue about how he was feeling.

Adeline waited until we were halfway up the big staircase before speaking, and even then she whispered. "Why was Uncle Braxton sending you off with Stone?"

"I don't know," I whispered back.

"He's up to something," she said as we came to the top of the stairs.

"What makes you say that?"

"Braxton never does anything without a reason. Neither does my father. The two of them have been plotting and scheming their entire lives."

"Is that why you offered to come along? To figure out what he was up to?"

We'd made it to the top of the stairs and had turned a corner in the hallway. "I mostly wanted to see how Braxton would react when I offered. He seemed to be orchestrating the trip—throwing the two of you together. I thought he'd make up an excuse why I couldn't go along."

"He didn't," I said.

"I know. I suppose I could have read it wrong."

I couldn't help but smile at that. "Maybe it's what he says it is—he simply wants me to like Alaska."

"Maybe…" She seemed to think hard. "I don't have all the pieces yet, but I know my uncle and my father. There's always more going on than meets the eye." She opened the door to a bedroom. "I vote you take this one. It's next door to me."

I looked around as I stepped inside the room.

It was hard to believe, but this suite was even bigger than the one I had now. It had a beautiful sitting alcove with a bay window that looked out onto the back of the house. To top it off, there was a balcony between the alcove and an identical alcove jutting out from the room next door. Below, I could see dozens of workers taking down the stage and the tents. I opened the door to the balcony and heard a backup alarm against the throb of a diesel engine.

"It's usually much quieter than this," Adeline joked over my shoulder.

"It's almost as big as my old apartment in Seattle."

"We want you to like it here," she said.

"I do like it here." I stepped onto the balcony, inhaling the fresh air and gazing at the now familiar view over the paddock to the mountain peaks.

If Braxton's secret plan was to make me like Alaska, he was well on his way to succeeding.

Seven

It was hard to believe it was possible, but Stone looked even sexier dressed in a flight suit than he did in blue jeans.

We were going up in a Cessna float plane, and I was excited. I'd never been in anything smaller than a commuter jet. I'd sure never taken off from or landed on water.

The blue-and-white Cessna was moored at a small wooden dock on the edge of Lake Hood. We'd arrived in a pickup, then the three of us lugged boxes and coolers and duffel bags from the truck to the dock. Leaning in through the open door, Stone had carefully stowed it all in the back, surrounding a single second-row seat next to the open door.

When he came through the door, he had a small duffel in his hands. "You'll have to hold this in your lap," he said to Adeline.

"I can take it," I offered. There was no reason why it had to default to her.

"You can't have it up front," he said. "It'll interfere with the flight controls."

Just then, another truck came to a stop on the laneway along the shore.

"It's Mason," Adeline said as Mason hopped out of the cab and gave us all a wave.

"I hope he's not thinking he'll come along." Stone scanned the tightly packed goods through the windows of the plane.

Mason came down the rise balancing a big box in his hands.

"What's up?" Stone called out.

I stepped to one side on the dock to give them both some room.

"Seafoam just called it in. They need to replace three extinguishers."

"What's the weight?" Stone asked. He took the box from Mason and hefted it to check.

"Ninety-seven pounds even."

Adeline shot her brother a frustrated look. "Are you kidding me?"

"You've been bumped," Stone told her.

Adeline shook her head, then slanted me a warning look.

I could see the wheels were turning on her suspicions, but I couldn't see this as a plot. Sometimes things just happened.

"Well, you two have a good time," she said in a flat voice.

"It's not like you haven't seen the sights before," Mason said to her.

"I know. I wanted to hang out with Sophie. She's fun. Not like you lot."

Mason and Stone both chuckled at her frustration.

I felt bad for her. "I could—"

"No," all three of them said at the same time.

"You're not staying here with me," Adeline said.

"You're not trading places," Stone said.

"You're going to have a great time," Mason said.

I gave up trying to be noble. "Oh… Well, okay then."

Stone hoisted the box onto the remaining back seat and settled the small duffel on top of it. Then he wrapped a strap over them both and fastened it down.

He repositioned the front passenger seat. "You're going to step on this," he told me, pointing to a small metal outcropping. "Hang on to the handle here. It's high, but I'll steady you from behind."

"Okay," I said, squaring myself with the door.

"We can talk when you get back," Adeline said.

I smiled. I was sure I'd hear theories about Braxton and Xavier, but I liked talking with Adeline. She was smart and funny and always a lively conversationalist.

I lifted my foot and reached up for the handle.

Stone bracketed my hips with his hands to steady me. He gave me a boost as I pulled myself up, ducking my head, twisting at the waist until I was sitting in the compact copilot's seat.

"Good?" he asked me.

I nodded.

He reached under the front of the seat. "Pull forward."

Just like a car seat, this one moved on rails, bringing me closer to the windshield and the controls.

"Keep your feet away from the pedals," he said. "They'll move. The door opens this way—pull up on the handle and push out." He demonstrated. Then he guided my hand under the seat. "There's a life jacket here if we go into the water."

"Excuse me?"

"It's a floatplane, Sophie. We'll be on the water."

"But not *in* the water."

"Not on purpose. But that's what the life jacket is for."

"This is not reassuring."

"Accidents do happen."

"Have you ever had one?"

"Not in a floatplane. A couple of hard landings on a bush strip, but nothing for you to worry about."

I wasn't really worried. Stone projected confidence and professionalism that put me at ease.

He disentangled a multistrap safety belt from beside my shoulder and put two straps over my chest. "These go in here." He inserted two small metal latches at my waist. "Then push like this. If you have to unbuckle, you just pull up on this. Got it?"

"Got it."

He tugged down on each of the straps and I felt securely lashed to the seat. Then he handed me a bulky headset with a microphone, and I put it on.

"Close to your mouth." He positioned the microphone. "Or I won't be able to hear you." His voice was muffled through the headset, but I understood. "All good?"

I nodded, the weight feeling strange as I moved.

Stone stepped back, and I noticed Adeline and Mason were still standing on the dock.

I smiled and waved to them again as Stone closed the door and cast off the ropes holding us to the dock.

Adeline snapped a photo.

I was glad she was memorializing my flight. I knew I'd be happy to have a picture of this adventure.

Stone went to the front of the plane and somehow crossed the floats, sliding down the far one before opening the pilot-side door and levering himself inside. He flipped some switches and moved knobs and levers, starting up the engine with a very loud roar. The plane rumbled beneath us as it bobbed in the waves.

Stone put on his headset, made some more adjustments, talked to the tower through the radio, and then he brought up the engine revs and we were moving out onto the lake.

"All set?" he asked through the headset with a grin.

"I am," I said back.

I was struck again by how sexy he looked in the khaki and green flight suit with a Kodiak Communications logo on the shoulder. A matching well-worn baseball cap shaded his eyes above a pair of sunglasses.

I wore sunglasses too, having been warned it would be bright in the sky.

Stone revved the engine further, turned the plane, made some more adjustments and sent us skimming along the waves. The plane went faster and faster until we tipped to one side. The movement startled me, and I held on. Then the second float lifted from the water, and the engine speed suddenly changed. The nose went up and we were floating on a cushion of air.

I looked out the side window as the shoreline and truck got smaller and smaller.

He banked the plane, so I was staring at the earth out my side window.

"Nice, huh?" His voice in my ears startled me.

"Nice," I agreed. It was stunning.

As we climbed higher, I could see the tall buildings of Anchorage. There were white-tipped mountains in the distance, and the ship-dotted water spread out far and wide. We headed for the ocean while Stone exchanged choppy information with the control tower.

"How long is the trip?" I asked after the tower went silent.

"Depends," he said.

"On...wind speed?" I gave it a guess.

"On how much you want to see along the way."

"Is there something I should see?"

"Many, many things."

"Then I'll let you decide." I settled back in my seat while Stone flew us off into the blue Alaskan sky.

Compared to commercial jets, we flew low and slow, making the detail of the world below us crisp and clear. We left the buildings of Anchorage behind and flew over the freighters and ships in the harbor before crossing a forest dotted with scattered lakes and populated with moose and caribou and even a few grizzly bears.

"I like the bears a whole lot better from up here," I'd said.

Stone had laughed at that.

We crossed a vast stretch of water to get to Kodiak Island. Then we followed an inlet, circling down to a long beach and a red-roofed log lodge surrounded by a bunch of smaller buildings. I could see a dock with two big floaters and assumed that's where we were aiming.

I got a little nervous as the water grew closer. Then we hit it with a jolt and immediately bogged down and slowed. Stone revved up the plane and turned us to the dock. As we lumbered up alongside one of the floaters, he stripped off his headphone and unbuckled, cracking his door open.

Then he shocked me by hopping out, quickly rounding the front of the plane across what I realized was a wire between the airplane floats before leaping onto the floater, a rope in his hand. He tugged the rope tight.

I sucked in a breath of surprise and relief. We were there.

I removed my headset and fumbled my way out of the

safety belt. By the time I got everything sorted out, Stone was opening my door and offering to help me down.

I slipped a little on the foot peg and he grasped me tight, turning and setting me down on the floater. I held on for an extra second, getting my legs stabilized as it rolled with the waves.

My hair blew around my face and I grabbed it up at the base of my neck, wishing I'd thought to put it in a ponytail.

While Stone finished securing the plane, I gazed at the beach and a second floater, where two big metal fishing boats were moored.

"Hello, Stone," a man's voice called from the top of a long ramp from the shore. It split at the bottom and connected the two floaters.

"Hey, Ray-Jay," Stone called back. He opened the back door of the plane and began hauling out the cargo.

I wanted to help, but it wasn't obvious what I should do, and I didn't want to get in the way.

"How's the fishing?" Stone asked.

Ray-Jay came onto the floater. "Fantastic. We're having a great year for salmon and cod, a few rockfish, which is nice."

"Lots of reservations?"

"Still booking up a couple of years in advance."

Stone grinned. "That's what you want."

Ray-Jay looked me over. "Hi, there. I'm Ray-Jay, general manager of Seafoam Resort."

"Also the owner of Seafoam Resort," Stone put in. "This is Sophie Crush."

"A special friend of yours?"

"A special friend of the family."

Ray-Jay's expression grew interested. "Oh, in that case, it's *very* nice to meet you, Sophie Crush."

He was about six feet tall and looked to be in his

midthirties, weathered and fit, his hair a little unkempt and his beard growth a few days old. He was a good-looking man, dressed in tan canvas utility pants and a green buttoned shirt with the sleeves rolled up.

He stepped closer, offering me his hand, and I shook with him, finding his grip strong and his palms callused. He might be the manager of the resort, but it was obvious he did a lot of physical work as well.

"Stand down, sailor," Stone growled at him.

"What stand down?" Ray-Jay looked at my left hand. "I don't see a ring. So, what are you, Sophie? Single, in a relationship, engaged to some dude who couldn't be bothered to buy you a diamond?"

"Uh…keeping my personal life private," I answered in a teasing tone.

Stone chuckled.

"Ouch," Ray-Jay said through his own laughter.

"We've only just met," I told him, happy to keep it light and joking. "Give a girl a chance to get to know you."

"That's not a no," Ray-Jay said.

"It's a no," Stone said. "We're only here for the afternoon." He turned back to his unloading.

"I sometimes get to Anchorage," Ray-Jay said to me. At the same time, he moved toward the open door of the airplane to help Stone.

"I live in Seattle," I told him.

My response seemed to stump him for a moment. "Seattle's an awfully long way away. Have you considered relocating?"

"She's not moving to Kodiak Island," Stone said. He climbed partway into the plane and handed a box out to Ray-Jay.

"We have the biggest spring salmon in the world," Ray-Jay said.

"Stop," Stone said. "You're annoying her."

"Am I annoying you?" Ray-Jay set the box down on the floater.

"You're amusing me," I told him honestly.

He gave a wounded groan.

Stone laughed from inside the plane as he pushed several boxes to the open door to Ray-Jay.

"That's not a bad thing," I said to Ray-Jay. "You have a good sense of humor. I like that."

"She likes that," Ray-Jay said to Stone, pulling out box after box and setting them down in a neat pile.

"She's brushing you off," Stone said.

"You don't think I know that? I'm not stupid when is comes to women. But she likes me. I'll take that."

I moved closer to the plane. "Can I help at all?"

"Nope," Ray-Jay said.

"We got this," Stone said.

I took a step back to clear the path.

"I'll call the boys to haul it all up to the lodge," Ray-Jay said. He pulled out his phone while Stone hopped down from the plane and shifted the last of the cargo to the floater.

"I feel quite useless," I said to Stone as he moved to my side.

"I didn't bring you along so you could work." He lightly touched the small of my back, urging me toward the ramp. It was fairly steep, and the beach came halfway down the dock, so I guessed the tide was out.

There was a double rope handle on either side of the ramp and the floor was rough, like sandpaper that gripped the bottoms of my hiking shoes. The wind was still brisk, so I used one hand on the stiff rope and kept the other around my hair.

We came to the top and crossed the dock, bringing us

onto a lush green meadow. A well-trod gravel path led to a gleaming log building, two stories high with a peaked roof and towering windows. It had a deck along one side overlooking the ocean and a tall stone chimney sticking out the top.

"This is really nice," I said, in awe that something this magnificent had been built in the wilderness. I'd seen from the air that there was no road access.

"Hungry?" he asked me.

My nose picked up the scent of fresh baked bread. "I am now."

"Good. Marianne will give us lunch, and then I've got some work to do."

"Anything I can help with this time?" I asked, hopeful, as we started up the path, a hundred yards or so to the main building.

"Got a background in data transmission or satellite tech?"

"Economics Degree from UW."

"Yeah?" Stone seemed impressed.

"Please don't tell me that surprises you."

"You don't seem like an economist."

"Not smart enough?" I'd admit there hadn't been an opportunity to demonstrate my business skills in Alaska.

"Not nerdy enough. You need a pair of glasses, a different color hair, maybe eyes that don't sparkle like you're up to something all the time."

"My hair is plain brown. And I'm not up to anything." Nobody had said that about my eyes before.

He seemed to study my hair. "It isn't brown. It's caramel with highlights of copper and gold. Haven't you ever seen it in the sun?"

I wasn't exactly buying his exotic description. "That sounds both expensive and delicious."

We came to a short staircase the led to a pair of double doors with big, multipaned windows. Stone touched the small of my back again. It was featherlight, gentlemanly. Even though I was perfectly capable of safely walking up a flight of stairs, I kind of liked it.

His fingertips were warm against my sky blue T-shirt. I knew there was an inch of bare skin between the shirt and my jeans, but he wasn't touching me there. I wished he would. I'd like to feel his rough fingertips brushing my bare skin.

A second later, he let me go, leaning around me to push open one of the wooden and glass doors.

It was nearly as bright inside as out with a wall of windows and multiple doors to the west side leading out to the deck. The floor was polished wood, gleaming a warm red and yellow. A reception desk and sitting area were at the front, with a comfortable-looking restaurant behind a partial stone wall.

"Stone!" A stocky woman of about fifty rushed forward.

Her cheeks were rosy, her hair neat and short, and she was wearing a black double-breasted tunic over a pair of gray slacks. She all but launched herself into Stone's arms and grinned as she gave him an enveloping hug.

"I heard you fly in." She smacked him on both shoulders as she let go. "Welcome back." Her attention then shifted to me.

I stepped forward, offering my hand. I wasn't usually into someone with that level of exuberance, but I found myself quickly caught up in Marianne's. "Sophie Crush. I'm up from Seattle, visiting the Cambridges."

She gave my hand an enthusiastic shake. "Nice to meet you, Sophie Crush. I'm Marianne. Welcome to Seafoam Resort."

I took another scan of the rooms surrounding us. "I'm blown away by all of this."

She smiled with what looked like approval. "Not what you expect out here, is it?"

"I don't know what I expected. Smaller for sure and more rustic."

"We get clients from everywhere. It's their trip of a lifetime, and we don't want to disappoint. The fishing is world-class."

"I saw the boats," I said.

"They just got back for lunch. Oops! I need to get back to the kitchen." She stepped away. "Make yourselves comfortable. It's clam chowder and salmon burgers today with chocolate cherry torte."

I loved the sound of chocolate cherry torte, and I hoped the bread I was smelling would be a part of the meal. Then I thought I might have to hike up a mountain or something after lunch to counteract the caloric intake.

The meal was every bit as delicious as it sounded. The buns were fresh baked, dense and chewy around flavorful salmon that Marianne said had been caught earlier in the morning. The dining room had filled up with a group of fishermen from New York City and another group who said they were from Berlin. Everyone ate hearty and seemed to be in a jovial mood.

They cleared out quickly after lunch, apparently heading back out for more fishing. Stone told me the staff processed and quick-froze the catch on-site so the guests could pack it home on dry ice and enjoy it all year long.

Stone and Ray-Jay left on four-wheel ATVs to drive up to a satellite station, while I spent the afternoon alone, happily wandering along the beach and around the property.

I found a sunny spot on the sundeck, where an attendant offered me a pair of binoculars.

I counted twelve bald eagles, saw countless birds and squirrels in the trees and even saw a deer and a fawn in the distance. To be fair, it was the friendly attendant who pointed out the deer and helped me train the binoculars on it. But I was still thrilled with the experience.

It was after five when I heard the ATV motors and watched Stone and Ray-Jay return them to a garage down the beach from the lodge. I'd discovered the garage, some sheds and equipment buildings tucked along the rocky beach east of the main lodge. On the west and south sides, the prettier parts of the property with a sandy stretch of beach, there were self-contained chalets dotted along the waterfront and among the trees.

I'd learned from a brochure in the lobby that guests could rent hotel rooms in the main lodge or they could choose more privacy with a two- or three-bedroom chalet. Gourmet meals, including wine and top-shelf drinks, were complimentary with either option. The Seafoam Resort was five-star all the way.

From where I sat now in a deep wooden Adirondack chair in a gazebo in front of the lodge, I watched Stone and Ray-Jay make their way up a dirt path.

Stone smiled when he saw me and gave me a wave.

I waved back.

Ray-Jay said something to Stone, and they both laughed.

I tried not to feel self-conscious. There was nothing that said they were talking about me. It could have been about anything.

"I hope you had a nice afternoon," Ray-Jay said as they approached.

"See everything?" Stone asked.

"I think so," I answered. "I saw a deer and a fawn."

"Good time of year for that," Ray-Jay said. "Did you get up to the river?"

I must have looked confused.

"The Seafoam Glacier River." Stone pointed up the mountain behind the lodge.

"We have a wildlife viewing platform over the valley."

"I saw them from the deck."

"You should take her up there," Ray-Jay said. He glanced at his watch. "It's a little early though—a lot more to see late in the evening."

Stone came inside and sat in the chair across from me. "Sound good to you?"

"It does." It sounded like fun.

"We can stick around and go up this evening."

I was surprised we had that kind of flexibility. Then again, it wasn't like it would get dark later.

"I'll let them know," Ray-Jay said as he headed for the lodge.

On the water below us, a couple of resort workers were scrubbing the floaters with long-handled brooms and big buckets of soapy water. They called back and forth to each other as they worked. Above us, a raven cried out, circling with three others above the rolling waves.

Stone stretched his legs and leaned back in the chair. He'd taken his flight suit off and wore a light T-shirt and a pair of black multipocket utility pants. He looked completely at home in the wilderness, tough and seasoned, although I knew he was only thirty-four.

"Do you travel to many installations?" I asked, picturing him flying all over Alaska in all kinds of weather.

"Not so much anymore. I've got a big crew now, so I stay in the Anchorage office most of the time. I miss it though. It's nice out here."

I remembered Adeline's suspicions about this trip. "Do you have a theory on why Braxton sent us?"

"I do," Stone said easily.

My curiosity perked up.

"It's not rocket science," he said. "He wants you to see some of Alaska."

There was a distinct contrast between Stone's interpretation of Braxton's motives and Adeline's.

"This particular part of Alaska," I probed. "Today, with you?"

"Why not this particular part of Alaska? It's a jewel in the crown, don't you think?"

"You don't think that's all it is?" I wasn't sure why, but I couldn't completely discount Adeline's perspective.

Stone considered me for a moment.

A gust of wind ruffled his dark, slightly unkempt hair, and I was reminded all over again that he was pure sexy.

"He feels guilty," Stone said.

"Because he was so suspicious of me?" Maybe a sight-seeing trip was Braxton's method of making up for that.

"Sophie, really?" Stone's tone and expression told me I was missing something simple.

I shrugged my shoulders and gave my head a little shake.

"Braxton left the hospital with the wrong baby. He left his own daughter behind."

"Oh." I hadn't thought about it from that angle.

For a split second I was glad my mother had missed all this. She might have felt the same way about leaving Emily behind, and that wouldn't have been fair. It wasn't her fault. Which meant, by extension, it wasn't Braxton's fault either.

"He's trying to make up for lost time," Stone said.

I felt a pinch of guilt. "I'm not making it easy, am I?"

Stone leaned forward in this chair. "It's not up to you to make it easy. Fact is, it's more his fault than yours, so he's the one who has something to make up for."

I shook my head while Stone spoke.

"None of this is on you, Sophie. No way, no how."

"It's not on him any more than it's on me."

"That would be a nuanced debate. Point is, he *thinks* it's his fault, so he's trying to make amends."

For the first time, I felt sorry for Braxton. Stone's words had a ring of truth.

"What should I do?" I was half wondering, half asking out loud.

"Nothing." He gestured with his hands to the scenery around us. "Enjoy."

He made it easy to feel better. I was enjoying myself. And Stone was a big part of the reason why.

It was well past eight o'clock when Stone pointed me to a four-wheeled ATV outside the resort's main garage.

"I thought we'd walk up," I said, thinking of the apple pie Marianne had served for dessert. It had come with ice cream and a slice of aged cheddar cheese. I'd eaten both.

"It's five miles," Stone said. "Distances are long around here."

Five miles uphill.

Stone swung his leg over the ATV and settled at the front of the long seat. "Hop on." He pointed behind himself. "Look for the footrests." He started the engine. "You can hang on to the back rack...or to me."

I saw his grin in profile. I put a hand on his shoulder and swung my leg over the seat, settling to get comfortable and finding the footrests.

The rack behind me did provide a convenient handle, so I hung on there. Snuggling up behind Stone and wrapping my arms around his waist seemed too intimate for the situation.

"Ready?" he asked.

"Ready."

He pulled ahead with a little lurch, turning us to go around the garage before picking up a dirt trail. We bumped a little on the uneven ground, but as we picked up speed the wind felt nice on my face. Earlier, Marianne had found me a hair fastener, and my high ponytail was much better than loose hair in the wind.

The fishermen had seemed tired during dinner, mostly settling into the lounge with their phones afterward or heading back to their rooms and chalets. Nobody else was interested in the trip up to the viewing platform.

The sky was still awash in sunshine, and moss-covered spruce trees towered above us as we climbed. Then we emerged from the trees onto the slope of a wildflower meadow covered with crimson fireweed, yellow poppies and blue lupine against the lush green grasses. Color flooded off in every direction.

We skirted a tiny glacier lake, then bounced our way over a rock-strewn trail, rounding a cliff face before we came to the platform. Railed and gated, it jutted out over a river valley about fifty feet below.

Stone pulled the ATV in a tight circle, parking it next to the gate, pointing down the hill. He shut off the engine, and the quiet boomed around us.

"Do you think we scared everything away?" I asked, taking in what looked like a deserted valley bottom as I climbed off the ATV, making room for Stone to dismount.

He left the ATV, flipped open a latch and pushed in a gate.

"They won't have gone far."

We walked onto the platform, where chairs were arranged in two groups facing the valley. There were six covered spotting scopes set along a narrow ledge with a row of cupboards below.

"Is it dangerous around here?" I asked, taking in the eight-foot chain-link fence on the trail side. It gave way to a much lower wooden railing out on the platform.

"It's mostly to give the tourists a sense of security. The bears aren't all that interested in us."

"Will we see more bears?" I looked around, deciding this might be my favorite way to see bears. It had been fun watching them lumber through the meadows from the airplane. But this vantage point would bring us much closer.

Stone removed the covers from two of the spotting scopes. "It's best to pick a spot and scan slowly."

I moved up to one of them.

"Pick a reference point up the river, then move your way down. This is the focus, and you can move it with the little lever here."

I moved my eye close. "It's all black."

"You have to take off the lens cover."

Light suddenly appeared in the scope.

"Oh. Thanks." I tried again, focusing, and I could make out an amazing level of detail on the shrubs and rocks and rushing water.

I scanned as Stone had suggested but didn't see anything that moved.

"Take a look here," Stone said, stepping back from his scope.

"What did you find?" I was already standing up to have a look. I squinted into the eyepiece. "A deer?"

It was a whole lot bigger than the deer I'd seen from the resort sundeck. Its head was crowned with an impressive rack of antlers. It bent forward to take a drink from an eddy on the river.

"That's an elk," Stone said.

"Is it big, or does it just look big from here? Wait." A rush of excitement went through me. "There's another, and another."

"They're fairly big, up to seven hundred pounds."

"That's plenty big. Are they grumpy?"

"They can be if you bother them. We're not going to bother them."

I moved back to my own scope. "How can I find them?"

"Go ahead and use mine. Watch for a while."

That didn't seem fair. He was the one who found them.

"Go ahead." He motioned. "I'll see what else I can find in yours. I've done this before."

I took the invitation because I was quite fascinated by watching the animals. But when I looked back, they were gone. "They left." I tried not to sound disappointed.

"Are you sure? Look closely."

I looked again, focusing, waiting. And then I saw a big brown shape. "Whoa."

"You see them?"

"I see what scared them."

"A bear?"

"Yes. No. Three bears." I watched as a big bear, a slightly smaller bear and a cub walked into the water, nosing around.

"Sow and a cub?"

I realized I was hogging the view and stepped back. "Go ahead."

"I'm good. You're having fun. Keep watching."

I hesitated.

"Seriously. I want you to have fun."

I tilted my head, squinting at him in mock suspicion. "Is Braxton paying you?"

"He is, but not to do this."

It was the first time that thought had entered my head. Why *was* Stone doing this?

I sobered. "I hope you know you don't have to be my tour guide."

"I know that."

"I mean, really."

"Really." He moved a little closer, and his voice turned hushed. "I like it when you're happy, Sophie." His gaze softened on me then. Or maybe it was the sunlight that had softened on his eyes. Everything suddenly felt softer, more intimate.

He moved closer still. He was going to kiss me, and I smiled at the idea.

"Happy," he repeated. His hand came up to my neck, fingers slipping against my hairline. He bent his head, put his arm around my waist and drew me forward.

"Happy," I echoed.

Our lips met, and just like it had all the times before, passion sizzled through me. I parted my lips. My arm slid around his neck. I leaned against him, pressing my other palm against his chest, feeling his strength and the echo of his heartbeat.

Our kiss grew deeper, and his fingertips found the seam between my shirt and my jeans. He touched my bare skin, and my whole being sighed in contentment. His hand splayed on my back beneath my shirt. Our thighs pressed together, and my back arched in desire.

He drew back ever so slightly, separated from me, then gave me a brief tender kiss on my swollen lips.

"Happy," he said, smiled and brushed my cheek.

"Happier," I said.

He stepped back farther. "You want to keep looking for animals?"

I was feeling far too restless to watch the elk and bears. "I'm done."

"Okay." He slipped the covers back on the scopes and we walked over to the ATV.

I didn't know what happened next, and I wasn't bold enough to ask. The last time I'd propositioned him, he'd turned me down flat. I didn't want to do that again.

He climbed onto the seat and started the engine.

When I climbed on behind him, he reached back, took my arms and drew them around his waist. I leaned in, snuggling up to his back, feeling his warmth, settling my hands on the flat of his stomach.

"Ready?" he asked.

I was beyond ready.

Eight

The ride back seemed disappointingly fast, much faster than the trip up. I gazed a little bit at the scenery, but mostly I focused on Stone. His shoulder was solid beneath my cheek, and the muscles of his stomach flexed as he steered the ATV around curves and obstacles, down steep slopes and through small creeks.

The sun was dipping below the horizon when the red roof of the resort came into view below us. But instead of taking the trail to the garage, Stone veered off on a little sideroad, coming to a halt in front of a pretty chalet.

I waited until he turned off the motor before lifting my head. "Are you picking something up?"

The windows were dark, and there were no signs of movement in the building. It was dead quiet and looked deserted.

"Can you hop off?"

"Sure. Are we walking to the dock?" I was a little tired, but I was up for it.

He turned on the seat and dangled a key from his left hand. "Ray-Jay gave this to me earlier."

I took in the key, then looked at the chalet. "We're staying?"

His eyes had a glow as he rose to his feet. "Yes."

"Together?"

"Well, there are three bedrooms if you're not—"

I stepped unhesitatingly up and grasped the front of his shirt. "I *am*," I said and kissed him.

He kissed me back, hard and deep, smiled, then kissed me again. "Good. Because I am too."

Hand in hand, we crossed the porch. The light was shadowed inside the chalet, dusk coming in through wide picture windows. I had a vague impression of two sofas, a fireplace, some landscapes on the walls and a kitchen nook at the back. But my attention was on Stone, his dark eyes, his strong sexy face, his fit body that I was already wrapping in my arms.

He kicked the door shut behind us, his breathing deep as he stripped off his shirt.

I did the same, thinking there was no point in waiting around on this. For good measure, I unhooked my bra and tossed it aside. Then I met him chest to chest, wrapping my arms around his neck, kissing his mouth. This time I knew we weren't stopping.

"Oh, man," he whispered between kisses. His warm palms splayed across my back. Then they rubbed and wandered, skimming beneath the waistband of my jeans, coming around to my stomach, moving up to my breasts.

"Oh," I groaned. "Yes." I tipped my head back and felt the sensation ricochet through me. Desire pooled at my core because Stone was magic.

I felt my way over his firm shoulders, his sculpted pecs,

along his washboard abs until I came to the waist of his pants, the fabric stiff and ungiving.

He cupped his hands under my rear and lifted me up.

My legs went naturally around his waist and our connection amped up my passion even through the layers of clothing.

He was moving then, walking forward, taking me backward until I felt a table come in beneath me. That freed up his hands, and he stroked my face, brushing back my hair and tenderly kissing my lips.

We stayed that way for a long time until he reached between us and unfastened my jeans.

I found the button at the top of his pants and did the same. Our gazes stayed glued to each other as we both shimmied out of our remaining clothes. And then we were naked and pressed back together.

Our kisses grew deeper. His hands roamed my body, and mine roamed his, touching, feeling, caressing as his breath quickened, and I could feel the deep thud of my heart pounding in my chest.

His caresses grew more intimate, and my need pulsed to life.

I scooted forward against his hand. My back arched and I moaned his name.

"Now?" he asked, the question more a growl than a word.

"Oh, yeah. Now is good. *Now.*"

It felt like he smiled, but my eyes were closed so I didn't know for sure.

Then he was with me, and we were one, and he thrust against me while his hands kept working their magic, finding spots I didn't know existed, pushing my passion to higher and higher heights.

The air grew hot around me, the rustle of leaves rose in volume.

Stone kissed my neck, then my shoulders, then my breasts. His labored breathing told me he was as into me as I was to him. It made me smile just as he returned to my mouth.

"Good?" he asked me, a smile in his own voice.

"Great," I told him. "So…very…great."

"Good," he said with a distinct shade of satisfaction. His thrusts become harder, faster, more insistent.

I gripped his shoulders as my body tightened into an endless spiral, colors flaring behind my eyes and an ocean's roar rushing through my ears.

"Stone," I gasped as the world contracted and pulsed within me.

"Sophie," he groaned in satisfaction, cupping my body, holding me tight and fast.

It felt like forever, but my breathing slowly grew shallow. Lethargy took over my limbs. It was good that Stone was still holding me, because I felt like I might melt into a puddle on the floor of the chalet.

I blinked my eyes open. They focused, and I looked around at cream-colored leather furniture, a rich burgundy rug, lovely oil lamps and vases, and a well-stocked bookshelf.

"Nice place," I said.

Stone chuckled, vibrating against me. The movement shouldn't have felt sexy, but it did. I had absolutely no desire to leave his arms, and my hold on him tightened.

He gathered me closer. His voice was muffled against my hair. "I like it here. I like it a lot."

When he drew back it was to run the pad of his thumb across my cheek.

I sighed, my face tilting for more.

He crossed my lips, and they tingled. They were thoroughly kissed but I still wanted more, so I kissed his thumb.

He paused for a brief second, then he kissed my mouth.

Passion stirred inside me, surprising me, and I reflexively squirmed against him.

He smiled against my lips. "You think?"

"Can we?"

"Oh, we can." He slanted his lips over mine, his tongue toying with me.

A bubble of passion grew and tightened inside me as waves of desire rose once more toward a crest.

We eventually found our way to a bed, a huge, soft, four-poster with a thick mattress and six fluffy pillows. We snuggled onto clean, crisp sheets.

Then we slept in each other's arms, waking in the morning when activity started outside around the resort. I wished we could stay longer on Kodiak Island, but I knew that was impossible. We were already late getting back, and I hoped it hadn't caused problems for anyone. Stone did have an important job, and I expected he'd been missed.

Marianne's breakfast was wonderful, and I stuffed myself again on her homemade bread, this time with wild blueberry jam. I raved so much about it that she offered me a jar to take back to Anchorage. I happy accepted the gift, looking forward to sharing it.

We eventually made our way back to the floater. The fishing boats were already out on the water, so it was quiet on the shore. Stone stowed a few things in the back of the airplane, but the load was a whole lot lighter this time, and the flight more direct.

Stone had left his truck at the Lake Hood base, so it was a quick trip back to the mansion, where Adeline was waiting to meet us.

"What did you think?" she asked, linking her arm with mine and steering me away from Stone.

"It was fantastic," I said.

"Pretty place, isn't it?"

"Yes, and delicious. And I loved the flight."

At first, I thought we were heading for the kitchen, but we took a right out onto the deck and closed the doors behind us.

The backyard was quiet again, barely a sign there'd been a party there just a couple of days ago. A gardener was at the far end on a ride-on mower. I'd discovered that grass and everything else grew incredibly fast in the long daylight hours of summer.

I'd have to tell Tasha about that phenomenon. Although after last night, the fast growing season in Alaska seemed like the second or third most interesting thing I had to share. I found myself smiling with the memory.

"Okay, now you really do have to tell me," Adeline said.

I realized she was watching my expression.

"Tell you what?" I put off my answer for a minute. I'd already decided I wasn't keeping it from her. I wasn't embarrassed about sleeping with Stone. Plus, she'd already guessed we were attracted to each other.

We stopped at a little furniture grouping in the sunshine. The cushions were hot, but they felt good, and a little breeze kept the air fresh.

"Spill," she said, kicking off her sandals and curling her legs beneath herself on the big comfy chair.

I did the same. "We saw moose and bears and caribou from the plane." I was teasing her, but it was pretty fun to watch her expectant expression.

"And…"

"And Kodiak Island is fabulous. You've been there, right? The food was off-the-charts. If I'd stayed much longer, I'd have gained five pounds."

"And…"

"And we went up to the viewing platform, saw a grizzly bear scare some elk."

"And…" She leaned toward me.

"And." I paused. "Yes, we did."

Adeline let out a little shriek, and I quickly glanced around to make sure nobody was in earshot.

"I knew it," she said in a whisper. Then she leaned closer still. "Give me all the details." She hesitated. "No, wait. Don't give me details. That would be weird. It's Stone we're talking about."

"I wasn't going to give you details."

She leaned back in obvious satisfaction. "I knew you were into him big-time."

She didn't know the half of it. Stone and I were positively combustible.

Adeline took on a pained expression and groaned. "Oh, man, your face. I so wish you could give me details."

We heard a door open and both looked over.

"I'm glad to see you back, Sophie," Braxton said as he and a younger man came out onto the sundeck. "Did you have a nice time?"

"The trip was wonderful." I didn't dare glance Adeline's way. "We saw all kinds of wildlife from the air and on the ground too. The Seafoam Resort is amazing."

"Stone said it was a success."

"You talked to Stone?" I was definitely not looking at Adeline now.

"I did. He says we can have the Seafoam Glacier installation upgraded in plenty of time. Sophie, this is Joe Breckenridge," Braxton said.

"Hello, Sophie. Nice to see you again, Adeline." Joe Breckenridge was tall with dark hair and a nice smile.

I guessed he was in his midthirties, in good shape, looked intelligent, was dressed quite formally for what

I'd seen of Alaskan men, wearing charcoal slacks and a steel gray sports jacket, his white collar open without a tie. His boots were practical though, sturdy brown hikers that looked like they'd seen a few miles.

"Joe." Adeline's response was curt, her tone anything but welcoming.

"You'll stay for dinner," Braxton said to Joe, clapping him on the shoulder.

"That's a tempting offer," Joe said. But his focus remained on Adeline as if he was trying to figure something out.

It was going to be my turn to pump her for information on this one.

"Not at all," Braxton said. "I appreciate you taking the time to talk in person while you're here in town."

"I wouldn't want to miss one of Sebastian's meals."

"He'll be happy to hear that."

"Sophie and I have dinner plans," Adeline said.

I shot a glance her way, immediately realized I looked puzzled and switched to a neutral expression.

Braxton's jaw tightened, but his voice remained even. "Can you postpone them?"

"We have a reservation."

"Change it."

"It's at The Big Edge, Uncle. You know how hard it is to get in there."

Joe extracted his phone from his inside jacket pocket. "I can help you out with that. What's a good alternate date."

I could see the offer threw Adeline, so I jumped in to try to save her. "I'm not sure how much longer I'll be staying."

That got Braxton's attention. "What? This is the first I'm hearing about you leaving."

"My house," I said, grabbing the first excuse that came to my mind. I figured I could back off on it later. "I have to get down there, at least for a while to get moved into the new house."

Braxton's eyes narrowed in suspicion, but he didn't call me on it. He turned his attention to Adeline, pinning her with the same glare he'd given me when I first announced the DNA results. "Please don't be rude."

"I'm—" She folded her arms over her chest and let out a huff. "Fine. We'll cancel."

Joe smiled, seemingly oblivious to the undercurrents, which was impossible, so he was faking it. He tapped something on his phone. "What day and time?"

Adeline didn't answer, still scowling.

"Friday," I suggested. "Seven o'clock." I figured there was no way he'd get a table, so we'd at least be off the hook for dining at The Big Edge, wherever that was.

"Hello, Rhonda," Joe said into the phone. "This is Joe Breckenridge calling. Can you possibly give me a table for Friday at seven?" He waited for a moment. "Sure. On the deck if you've got it, near the fireplace?" He paused again. "Yes, I will. Thanks." He disconnected. "Done."

I was shocked. Who was this guy?

"He's a Member of Congress," Adeline said after Braxton and Joe left the sundeck. "You want a drink? It's only two, but we could have a mimosa, pretend it's part of brunch."

"As in the United States Congress?" I asked.

Adeline came to her feet. "Yeah, that Congress. You want a scone or something to go with it?"

"Sure," I said, standing. "He's pretty young to be in Congress."

"His family owns the biggest ranch in Alaska. They've been here for generations. Joe went to Harvard Law, and he thinks he's the stuff."

We started across the sundeck to the kitchen.

"He's a lawyer?" He did strike me as the lawyer type.

"That's how some get into politics."

"You don't like him." I stated the obvious.

"I don't really know him."

I wasn't buying it. "Come on, your reaction to him was extreme."

Adeline stopped with her hand on the kitchen door handle. "Sophie." Her tone was patient with just a touch of exasperation that I didn't think was directed at me. "Here's the thing. Braxton and my dad want influence across the state and beyond. They have enormous plans for Kodiak Communications, and they want to launch a family dynasty along the way. Who better to pull into the fold than a congressman?"

A light bulb flashed on in my brain. "Oh."

She opened the door wide. "Yeah, *oh*. Mimosa?"

"You bet." I followed her into the kitchen, leaving the door open and letting the fresh air follow us inside.

From one of two double-doored refrigerators, she pulled out a pitcher of orange juice and a bottle of champagne.

I took a moment to marvel at the kind of household that had random bottles of champagne just sitting in the fridge for anyone to use. It was a good label too. I recognized it from working at The Blue Fern.

"Glasses are third cupboard from the end." Adeline pointed.

"He's not your type?" I asked as I extracted a pair of stemless champagne flutes. They were beautiful blown crystal, with a heavy base and a tapered oblong shape.

"He's a politician."

"That's a dealbreaker for you?"

"Yes. And even if it wasn't, or even if he was just a plain old lawyer, I'm not going to let my dad and his scheming brother get away with programming my life for their advantage. There's a reason I've spent nine years at school in California."

I held up the glasses. "These?"

"Perfect."

I pushed the cupboard closed with my elbow. "So, you're not there for the love of urban planning?"

"I do love urban planning. And I really like California. I like Alaska too, but coming back for too long has its problems. As you just saw." She popped the cork on the champagne bottle, and it flew into the air, hitting the ceiling then bouncing off the counter before settling on the tile floor. She scooped it up.

"Are you sure it's all about you?" I set down the glasses and poured orange juice into each of them.

There was dry laughter in Adeline's voice as she wiped the errant bubbles from the outside of the bottle. "Oh, I'm sure. My dad and Braxton are bulldogs, not particularly subtle."

"How does Joe feel about it?"

"I'm the daughter of a prominent businessman, in the technology industry no less, who was born and raised in Alaska and is of marriageable age. I know how to dance and how to schmooze and I dress up decently for formal occasions."

"You'd look beautiful on formal occasions."

She had the kind of leggy figure that looked great in absolutely everything. Plus, her auburn hair was dramatic, and her green eyes were unique. If I was Joe, looking for a great Alaskan political bride, Adeline would be my first choice.

"I'd do it if I was him," I said.

"Do what?" She topped up each of our glasses with bubbly champagne.

The drinks looked delicious. And there was a basket of fresh cranberry scones on the counter.

"Marry you if I was Joe," I said as I took one of the mimosas and helped myself to a napkin and a scone.

Adeline laughed so suddenly, I thought she might spill her mimosa. "*You*, I'd marry."

"Then again, we're cousins."

"Good point." She shrugged then, heading for the door. "But we've wandered way off topic."

She was right about that.

As we found our chairs again, the horses whinnied in the distance. A small herd of them galloped across the extended paddock, and I wondered if something had scared them. I'd asked Stone if bears bothered them, but he said they were safe in a herd.

"You're not really leaving soon, are you?" Adeline asked as we sat down.

"I haven't given it much thought lately." I realized it was true. I had settled in at the mansion, staying focused on the day-to-day instead of planning very far ahead. Maybe because nothing was calling me from Seattle. "My best friends, all three of them, moved away from Seattle last year."

"Do you miss them?"

I set the scone on the low round table in front of us and took a sip of my mimosa. It was delicious. "I do, especially Tasha. The other two, Layla and Brooklyn got married first to twin brothers."

"Really?"

"Yeah, it's a little strange seeing the four of them together. I can't tell the men apart until they hug or kiss their wives."

Adeline laughed and broke off a piece of her scone, popping it into her mouth.

"But they're really happy. Tasha and I were left behind, so we spent a lot of time together last year. But then she took up with James, Layla's brother, and they moved to LA."

"So, you have friends in LA?"

I nodded. Then I took a bite of my scone, and it melted in my mouth. "These are fantastic. How does Sebastian not own his own restaurant?" The chefs I'd met in Anchorage so far were beyond impressive.

"Because we pay him so much to stay here."

"Really?"

"I don't know the exact figure, but whenever he muses about expanding his horizons, the family panics, and somebody ups his salary."

"I don't blame you. But I hope he's happy."

Stone strolled through the open kitchen door. "Hope who's happy? Me?"

Adeline rolled her eyes. "Sebastian."

"Why wouldn't Sebastian be happy?" he asked, taking one of the chairs in the grouping.

"I thought he might want to open a restaurant," I said.

Stone stared at me for a second. "Are you trying to steal Sebastian?"

"What? Me?"

"Are you going to open a restaurant."

"No."

"Here in Alaska?" he asked.

"I said no."

"That's a great idea," Adeline said. "But maybe you should do it in California. You know, to be closer to your friends." She gave a cunning smile. "Sacramento is nice."

"Don't you try to steal Sophie," Stone warned her.

"I'm not a trading good," I answered back.

"It's up to Sophie," Adeline said. "But Sacramento is a whole lot warmer than Alaska in January."

"You both know I'm not opening a restaurant, right?"

"We'd outbid you for Sebastian anyway," Stone said. "Any more of those scones left?"

"In the basket," Adeline said.

Reminded, I savored another bite of my scone while Stone went to the kitchen to get one for himself.

"Does he know I know?" Adeline whispered while he was gone.

I shook my head.

"Okay," she said. "Mum's the word."

It wasn't a deep dark secret. Then again, I'd prefer it if the entire family didn't discuss my sex life.

"I see Joe's here," Stone said as he sat back down. He'd poured himself a mimosa as well. "The three of them are holed up in the den."

"Some coincidence," Adeline said.

"That they're in the den?" Stone asked.

"That Joe Breckenridge showed up right now."

Stone grinned. "He's a decent guy. You should give him a chance."

"Not on your life."

"Are you in favor of matchmaking?" I asked Stone, a little surprised that he knew and a little surprised by his acceptance of the interference in Adeline's life.

He shrugged. "There are all kinds of ways to meet people."

"I'm not chattel," Adeline said, clearly annoyed.

"You're having a knee-jerk reaction," he said.

"To being paraded in front of a suitable match for the convenience of the family corporation?"

"It's more than just that."

"Whose side are you on?" I asked Stone. Adeline clearly

wasn't interested in Joe. Why would anyone want to push her there?

"There are no sides," he said. "Just a family who loves her and a man who's attracted to her."

I squared my shoulders. "What about a woman who knows her own mind?"

"Yeah," Adeline said, pointing to me. "That."

"I'm only suggesting you—" Stone turned to include me in his answer "—*she* give the guy a fair shot."

"He's a congressman," Adeline said, her tone laced with disgust.

"And I'm a vice president." Stone took a drink of his mimosa.

I really didn't get the comparison.

Adeline came to her feet. "Want another scone?" she asked me.

"No, thanks. I'm good." They were delicious but filling.

As she walked away, I opened my mouth to ask Stone why he was pushing Adeline.

"Hey," he said, interrupting my question, shifting closer, his smile soft, his blue eyes warm and welcoming. "How're you doing?" It was as if our debate had never taken place.

"Fine." I gave in to his change in mood because I didn't really feel like arguing. Plus, I was fine, very fine with warm memories of Stone from last night and this morning.

"You want to do something?" he asked.

"Like what?"

"I don't know. Head into town, dinner, dancing."

"Are you asking me on a date?"

"Yes, I'm asking you on a date. Want to go on a date?"

Adeline's footsteps sounded on the deck as she made her way back to us.

"Sure," I said quickly before she arrived.

"Sophie still needs a new vehicle," Adeline said as she sat back down. "It really is silly to keep that rental car."

I hadn't wrapped my head around that idea yet— buying something that would sit idle for so long. I did intend to come back to Alaska for visits. But I didn't know when, and I didn't know for how long.

"Sophie's used to a different kind of lifestyle," Stone said.

"A lifestyle without cars?" Adeline asked as she sat down. "Do you take transit, or surely you don't Uber it all over Seattle?"

"I have a car at home," I said.

"A normal lifestyle where people have to save up to buy things like cars," Stone said.

Adeline looked confused. "She doesn't have to pay for it herself."

"I can easily pay for it myself." I could pay for it with this week's royalties alone.

She shot Stone a look of incomprehension. "So, what's your point?"

I decided to be blunt. "I'm having trouble getting used to being rich."

"You mean getting used to being a Cambridge?"

"Sophie has her own money," Stone said. "A lot of money."

"Recently," I clarified.

"Oh, right, the invention," Adeline said.

"She worked for every penny. The dessert machine, Sweet Tech, was very valuable."

"That's fantastic!" Adeline rocked to her feet. She reached down and polished off the last of her mimosa. "Then let's head down to the dealership. This is going to be fun."

Nine

Adeline had ushered me into a luxury car dealership while extolling the value of long-term comfort, looks and quality over short-term price savings. Stone had brought up the rear, agreeing with everything she said. In the end, I'd decided on a midsize metallic blue crossover that, I had to admit, I absolutely loved. Coached by Adeline, with Stone dismissing each of my objections, they'd talked me into taking one that was already on the lot and loaded with options and extras.

I'd driven it back to the mansion with Adeline in the passenger seat, arriving in time for the dinner with Joe Breckenridge.

Her bedroom was next door to mine, and we shared the balcony. Since we both liked fresh air, we kept our balcony doors open much of the time and had taken to going back and forth that way.

She breezed into my room. "What do you think?"

I finished pulling a sweater over my head and looked at her.

She did a twirl in a bright white pullover blouse with fine mesh on the upper chest and cap sleeves. It was snug and silky over a pair of black skinny jeans with a pair of midnight blue leather boots. Her earrings were gold and chunky, and her makeup looked brighter than normal.

"What are you doing?" I asked.

"What do you mean?"

My sweater was deep purple with a bit of sparkle to it, three-quarter sleeves and over a pair of blue jeans. I'd planned to wear flats.

"You're all dressy."

She looked down at herself. "Not that much. We're eating in the formal dining room."

I checked myself out. "Should I change?"

"You look great."

I decided I'd at least wear some boots with heels and rebrush my hair. "Are we going formal because he's a Congressman?"

"Because Dad and Uncle Braxton think the sun rises and sets on him. And I don't want any grief from them later on for supposedly shirking my family duty."

"Then I'm at least changing my pants." I popped the button and unzipped.

I'd brought some black pants with me that would work, plus a pair of tapered heel ankle boots. And I was definitely upgrading my earrings.

"They won't fuss about you," she said.

I took the pants from my bottom drawer and slipped them on. "So it's the matchmaking thing?"

Adeline gave her hair a toss. "They'll pretend it's something else, like a lack of respect, yada, yada. But I know what's really going on."

"Uh-huh." Sophie was starting to think Adeline was protesting a little too much. She watched me for a moment. "I don't suppose there's someone at the table *you* want to impress."

I couldn't keep myself from smiling. "I don't think he's fussy about what I wear."

"If anything at all," she said with a gleam in her eyes.

"It's dinner," I said in a mock rebuke.

I brushed out my hair and switched my gold stud earrings for a pair of smooth purple crystals dangling in braided silver. Then I pulled on the boots and did my own pirouette.

"We look amazing," Adeline said.

"We'll definitely dress the place up."

"Make sure you sit beside me. I don't want to get stuck in the business talk all night long."

"Were you ever interested in the family business?" Other than Adeline, all the members of the family were intimately involved in Kodiak Communications. She seemed to quite studiously avoid it.

"Never."

"Why not?"

"I'm not technologically inclined. I'm not interested in being on the sales force. And, most of all, I'm not going to spend the rest of my life under my father's thumb."

"Is he really that bad?" My impression of Xavier so far was that he was a lot like Kyle, easygoing and carefree.

"Passive-aggressive."

"How so?"

"He makes suggestions on what I should do, where I should go, how I should feel. And if I don't take them, he frowns."

"Frowns?" That didn't sound so bad to me.

"Then he makes them again…and again. Then he reframes them, thinking he's being sneaky. Oh, and he always brings Braxton in on pressing me, plus Mason and Kyle. I don't think my brothers are malicious about it. They just listen to his logic—which is always well planned out by him and Braxton—and then they ask me why I'm being so stubborn." She opened the bedroom door to the hallway.

"Give me an example," I said as we started for the dining room.

"Joe Breckenridge."

"I already know about him. What else?"

"University of Alaska instead of California. My major. My prom dress. My prom *date*."

"Did they try for Joe?" I joked.

"Joe came later. They didn't know he'd rise like he did, otherwise…" She pulled an exasperated expression.

We laughed together as we came to the bottom of the stairs.

The formal dining room was at the front of the house off the great room. Its dramatic oblong table was usually surrounded by eighteen comfortable chairs. It was shortened tonight and set up for eight. Braxton and Xavier were talking alone, while Stone, Mason and Kyle engaged Joe in what looked like a lively conversation while they sipped something amber in heavy crystal glasses.

"Ah, *there* they are," Xavier said.

Something in his tone had me glancing at Adeline. Were we being rebuked for tardiness? I hadn't known there was a set time for the dinner.

Adeline gave my forearm a surreptitious squeeze.

"Welcome, ladies," Braxton said. He came partway to greet us. His gaze on me, he pulled out a chair. "Please," he said.

It was pretty clear I didn't have a choice of where to sit.

Xavier had done the same thing directly across the table. "Adeline?"

"I was going to sit next to Sophie."

"Don't be silly," Xavier said smoothly. "Sebastian has it all planned."

Adeline gave me a knowing look as we separated.

I sat down on the springy seat and Braxton gallantly pushed in my chair.

"Thank you," I said over my shoulder.

Stone took the seat to my right, closest to the head of the table, while Mason sat on my left. Joe sat down opposite Stone and Kyle settled across from Mason. Braxton and Xavier took the ends of the table that had been set to fit the gathering.

A man in a suit jacket—I guess I'd call him the head-waiter—immediately emerged from a side door. He was followed by eight others in black slacks, white shirts and vests. It struck me as overkill, significant overkill.

The headwaiter spoke up. "Good evening, everyone. Tonight's dinner will be honey Dijon scallops, followed by a charred citrus salad. Pan-seared halibut with plum and cucumber, accompanied by wild mushroom risotto will be the main course, with a crème brûlée for dessert. For the red tonight, Sebastian suggests a 2007 Napa Cabernet Sauvignon from Chateau Black. For the white, a 2013 Hilltop Vineyards Chardonnay."

I was growing hungrier by the second.

"Ladies?" Braxton looked to me first. "Red or white?"

"Red, please." I suspected either of them were going to be spectacular.

"White, thank you, Randall." Adeline said.

Randall gave a subtle hand signal and a waiter stepped up behind Adeline. It took me a second to realize another waiter had stepped up behind me and was reaching past to fill my wineglass. Another waiter deftly removed my white wineglass.

I'd always thought The Blue Fern had offered gracious service. But these guys had us beat by a mile.

"Gentlemen?" Xavier asked.

Around the table, each of the men stated their wine preference. Stone went with red. Joe and Adeline were the only ones drinking white.

I leaned closer to Stone while several waiters poured, keeping my voice low. "Is this how the rich do it?"

"Sometimes," he replied in an undertone.

"It's unnerving."

"Just roll with it."

"How's the family, Joe?" Xavier asked as the waiters all finished and withdrew.

"Dad's good," Joe answered. Then he smiled. "Mom's on him to let the ranch manager take over more work so they can travel, but I don't think he's interested."

"He should think about it," Braxton said. "Family has to come first."

I took a first sip of my wine. It was fantastic.

"I'll tell him you said so," Joe answered with a wry smile. "But I doubt it'll do any good."

"Your sisters?" Xavier asked.

"Patty's pregnant again, and Elaine's dating a guy from Texas."

"You have sisters?" I asked Joe. I don't know why, but Joe had struck me as an only. Maybe that was me listening to Adeline's opinion.

"Just the two of them, no brothers though. Elaine's Texas guy is from a ranching family."

"Your dad will be happy if that works out," Xavier said.

"And we all know *that's* important," Adeline said, stopping the conversation.

"I don't have any sisters or brothers," I put into the silence. "These new cousins are who I have now, of course, and I'm super excited about that." My words beat Adeline's for stunned silence, and I quickly realized my mistake. I swallowed. "I assumed you'd told him."

"Why?" Mason asked in obvious surprise.

"Are we telling people?" Braxton looked pleased.

"Close friends and family," I answered hesitantly. I'd already told Tasha.

Joe sent a warm smile my way.

Adeline frowned.

"I'm immensely honored to be included in that group." Joe looked to Braxton. "What is it you didn't tell me?"

Braxton set down his wineglass and sat up straighter, squaring his shoulders. "Sophie—" he gave me the warmest smile I'd ever seen "—is my daughter."

Joe kept a straight face, but I could see the shock in his eyes.

"We better tell him the whole story," Stone said.

Joe looked to Stone, but it was Mason who spoke up. "Emily and Sophie were switched at birth."

"At the hospital," Stone added. "It was a terrible mix-up that we only just figured out."

Now Joe peered at me, assessed me. "You're…"

I raised my glass. "Part of the family."

"She sure is," Braxton said in an overly hearty voice. It lent credence to Stone's assertion he was feeling guilty.

Kyle raised his glass my way. "Welcome, Sophie."

Everyone followed suit, and I felt extremely self-conscious.

Stone gave me a squeeze on the thigh. "Just go with it," he whispered again.

I was also rolling with my new SUV, sitting in the driver's seat with the thick owner's manual in my hands. I was in part simply marveling that it was all mine—since I'd never owned a brand-new vehicle before. But I was also having fun learning how everything worked, like how to add Bluetooth to the sound system and adjust the seat heaters. It was plenty warm now, but if I came back to Alaska in the winter, I was going to appreciate having a hot back and a toasty rear end.

The passenger door opened, surprising me. I looked up to see Braxton.

"How do you like it?" he asked, bending to peer inside.

"I like it a lot." I'd promised myself to be more patient with him. I didn't hold him responsible for the hospital mix-up, and the situation was clearly difficult for him too.

He gestured to the passenger seat. "Do you mind?"

"Sure," I said, and he slid inside, closing the door behind himself.

"I'm learning about the heated seats," I said to keep the moment from becoming silent and awkward.

"You'll like those. Have you tried the remote start?"

"I did," I admitted. I'd played with it a few times, shutting the SUV on and off from across the driveway.

"You'll like that in the winter too. We can clear out a spot in the garage for you."

"There's no need."

"Happy to do it. Saves you from having to brush off all the snow."

"Okay. Thanks." I told myself to be gracious. Maybe I would be back in the winter. And who wouldn't prefer to park in a garage at thirty below?

He affectionately patted the blue dashboard. "Were you thinking about taking it out for a spin?"

I nodded. That had been my plan. "Would you like to join me?"

"I'd like that." He looked pleased by the invitation.

Though I still wasn't sure of my feelings about him, I knew spending some time alone together was a good idea.

I took a breath and pressed the start button. The engine revved right up.

"Sounds good," he said.

I hadn't yet got used to the size compared to my compact car, and the SUV felt large as I pulled down the driveway toward the road.

But it was smooth on the gravel, and very quiet inside. It was a little too quiet with Braxton sitting next to me. So I tuned in a local radio station, glad I'd looked up how to work the sound system.

"I pulled out a few photo albums for you," he said as I turned left on the road.

"That was nice of you."

"I thought you might like to see some more pictures of your mother."

I chafed a bit at the description and felt my jaw go tight.

"Would you rather I called her Christine?" he asked kindly, obviously attuned to my expression.

I would, and I told myself to be honest with him. "When I hear the word *mother*, I think of my real mother… Sorry, I mean, the mother who raised me."

"Don't apologize. Christine it is then."

"Does that bother you?" I glanced his way but couldn't read his expression.

"It's not about me," he said, but his gaze stayed forward, staring out the windshield.

I could acknowledge her as the stranger who was my biological mother, but that was as far as I could go right now.

"Have you been down to the marina yet?" he asked.

"On Lake Hood?" I assumed he meant the one next to the floatplane dock.

"There's a smaller one at the marine park," he said. "It's just up ahead, through the lookout."

I shook my head. I could see the lookout coming up.

"We have a sailboat moored there if you're interested."

I'd never been sailing, but what I'd seen of the sport looked like fun.

"I wouldn't mind taking a look." I'd admit to feeling more comfortable with a focus and a destination than to driving aimlessly along making conversation.

"Turn into the lookout," he said.

I slowed my speed and hit my signal, even though there was nobody else on the road to see it. Then I pulled into the big gravel semicircle.

"Straight through," he said, pointing ahead.

I hadn't seen it from the main road, but there was a narrow road leading out the opposite side of the pullout.

"It's better if you use four-wheel drive."

"Is this a test of me or the SUV?" I asked in a joking tone.

"It's not a test. The road's just bumpy and steep."

I shifted the knob to four-wheel drive.

The road twisted through the fir trees and the under-brush. I slowed my speed, avoiding the worst of the boulders and potholes.

Soon, the road leveled off and smoothed out. We took a sharp turn and the forest disappeared behind us. We'd come out at a beach, more a marina than a park, with a rocky shore, a small parking lot and a grid of docks berthing about forty different boats. They ranged from twenty-footers to something that looked like forty or so feet. Some had sailing masts, others were obviously pleasure yachts. I didn't see any fishing boats.

"You can park anywhere," Braxton said.

I pulled to the edge of the lot where I thought I'd be out of the way of other traffic.

"You sail?" I asked as we started for the dock.

I was guessing he must. Sailing took a lot of skill and

practice, but who better than rich people to have the time to learn? Not to mention the money for lessons and up-keep of a sailboat.

The breeze was brisk by the water, but I'd learned to pack a hair tie everywhere I went, so I pulled my hair into a snug ponytail. It was a warm day, so the wind was re-freshing against my bare arms.

Braxton settled a ball cap on his head. "Do you sun-burn?"

"I tan pretty easily."

"That's good. This way."

We crossed the gravel patch to a dock that led out to the rows of wharfs. I speculated on whether the Cambridges owned a little dinghy for day fun in the waves or some-thing more exotic and luxurious.

As we kept walking, the answer became obvious. The *Emily Rae* was the biggest sailboat in the marina. It was gleaming white with a long center mast, dual benches on deck that wrapped around the helm. There was a man on board wearing white slacks and a pale blue shirt.

"Morning, Mr. Cambridge," the man called out.

"Morning, Wade. This is my daughter, Sophie."

If Wade had a moment's pause at meeting a full-grown daughter of Braxton's, he didn't show it.

"Good morning, Ms. Cambridge," he said.

"It's Crush, but Sophie's fine."

"Then good morning, Sophie. You're welcome to come aboard."

There was a small gangplank connecting the sailboat to the dock, and he held out his hand.

I was more than happy to take a tour. I'd never been on a sailboat before.

"Do we have time?" I asked Braxton. My morning was clear, but he was a busy man.

"All the time in the world," he said, looking happy that I'd agreed.

He followed me on board, and the boat rocked gently on the waves beneath our feet.

"Any trouble with motion sickness?" Wade asked me.

I shook my head. "Never have."

"Good." He shaded his eyes and looked across the bay. "It's not too bad out there today."

Out there? I felt a shimmer of excitement at the prospect of skimming over the bay.

"It's only a quick hop to Fiddler's Point," Braxton said to me.

"There's a pretty trail on the island if you'd like to stretch your legs," Wade added.

"Am I keeping you from something?" I asked Braxton.

"Not a thing."

Wade grinned.

"What can I do to help?" I asked him. I didn't know much about sailing, but I knew it took work to crew the boat.

"You can enjoy the ride," Wade said. "Let me get you a life vest. Do you have sunglasses?"

I didn't. I hadn't planned to go far. "No."

"No problem. We've got spares." He disappeared, ducking his way down a short staircase middeck.

"This is amazing," I said to Braxton, looking around at the shore, the surf and the few other boats skimming past. Seagulls swooped and cried above us, while the wind whistled past and the waves slapped rhythmically against the hull.

Braxton's gaze was soft. "I'm so glad you like it."

Wade returned with three black-and-yellow life vests plus a white baseball cap and a pair of sunglasses for me.

We shrugged into our outfits and buckled up.

Braxton handed Wade his phone. "Can you get a shot of us?"

Wade took the phone and motioned us into the center of the deck in front of the mast.

I braced myself in case Braxton wrapped an arm around my shoulders, not sure how I'd feel about a hug from him. But he didn't. Instead, he took half a step back and shifted behind my shoulder to better fit in the frame. Wade then snapped a couple of quick shots, handed the phone back to Braxton and deftly cast us off.

We chugged out a fair distance using a quiet motor before Wade and Braxton let out the sails. In mere moments Wade was back at the wheel and we were skimming faster and faster across the waves. The boat canted to one side, but I felt perfectly safe hanging on to the rails.

The wind blew against my face, water spraying up, cooling me in the warm sun.

Braxton sat down next to me.

"Do you sail yourself?" I asked, thinking my earlier assumption could have been wrong. Maybe the rich didn't have to learn how to sail, since they had the money to hire people to do it for them.

"Sometimes, more when I was younger. Now, Stone, Mason and Kyle are the keeners."

"Stone sails?" As soon as the question was out, I realized my mistake. I should have included Mason and Kyle in the question. "I mean, as well as flying floatplanes."

"Flying and sailing use a lot of the same principles," Braxton said, making a motion with the flat of his hand in the breeze. "A sail is just a wing of a different nature."

I hadn't thought of it that way before. But I could see what he meant. I gazed up at the bright sail billowing in the breeze. "It pulls instead of lifts."

He looked pleased. "That's right."

"Do you spend a lot of time on the water?" I asked.

He seemed at peace out here.

"Not as much as I used to do." He closed his eyes and seemed to savor the motion. "I miss it."

"It's very calming."

"It is on a day like this," Wade noted. "But we have some rough ones too. Days when the weather changes on a dime. Then it gets adventurous."

I checked out the few clouds, the breeze through the trees on shore and the roll of the waves. "Is it going to change today?" I wasn't sure I was ready for adventurous.

"Probably not," Wade said.

"The forecast is good," Braxton said. He opened his eyes. "It should be smooth sailing." He seemed to appreciate his own joke.

It was such a typical dad joke, so I smiled with him.

"Can I look below?" I asked, still curious to see what was down there.

"By all means," Braxton said. He rose and gestured for me to go first down the narrow stairs.

I ducked my head and blinked my eyes to adjust them to the change in light, pulling off my sunglasses to improve my view. It was compact down here, but it looked efficient, streamlined and gleaming clean.

Royal blue benches curved around the perimeter. There was a dinner-height table in between them, a tiny sink and kitchen area directly beside me, and a door to a berth at the far end. There were narrow porthole windows on each side.

"Head's through here," Braxton said, tapping a door opposite the kitchen. "Twin berths behind us. We can sleep six, well three couples. The beds aren't the biggest in the world."

"So, you could do a multiday trip?"

"Sure can."

"This is impressive."

"It's compact, but we've got a lot of use out of it over the years."

"It's bigger than I expected." I scooted around the table and took a look inside the front berth. It seemed like it would be better for kids than adults with the way it narrowed at the foot. You'd have to snuggle up close to your sleeping partner to get two adults in there. I thought briefly of Stone and smiled.

I took a look at the aft berths next. They were bigger and looked comfortable. I couldn't help but wonder if I might have a chance to take an overnight trip someday. My thoughts went to Stone again and curling up with him while the waves rocked us.

When we went back up into the sunshine, we were halfway across the bay, heading straight for a spit of land on the opposite shore.

"Is that Fiddler's Point?" I asked.

"That's it," Wade answered as Braxton sat down.

I noticed a woodgrain walkway around the bow of the boat. It was narrow but surrounded by a thin railing. I pointed. "Okay to walk up there?" I pictured myself leaning into the wind at the tip of the bow.

"Sure," Braxton said. "Hang on to the rail. But if you fall in, don't worry. We'll circle back and pull you out."

I checked his expression to see if he was joking. I couldn't tell, but I wasn't afraid of falling. The rail looked sturdy, and we were steady on the water. I grasped the smooth wet rail and stepped up.

"She's a natural," Wade said behind me.

I liked the idea of being a natural. Maybe I'd learn the basics of sailing someday. Maybe Stone would teach me. He'd suggested a dinner date, maybe it could be a sailing picnic instead of a restaurant meal.

I made it out to the bow and steadied myself in the tri-angle of the rail. The wind was fresh, filled with salt spray and hitting my face head-on. I grinned and gazed at the shore as it came closer and closer.

Wade called out to me. "I can dock here if you'd like to walk up to the waterfall."

I was intrigued but still worried about the time. I turned and made my way back, hopping down to join Braxton on the bench seat. "You're sure I'm not keeping you from anything?"

"I'm enjoying myself," he answered. Then he gave Wade a nod and rose to help.

My phone pinged in my pocket, surprising me, since cell service was spotty outside Anchorage. I would have guessed we might be too far offshore.

I checked, expecting Adeline, but it was Tasha.

Can you talk? was her message.

Call you later? I responded. I'm on a sailboat.

With that Stone guy?

With Braxton.

Interesting... Hope it goes well! Later!

I signed off with a thumbs-up emoji and tucked my phone back into my pocket.

The boat lurched as we touched against a rather broken-down wharf and rocked side to side.

Wade hopped off with a rope in his hand and quickly tied us off.

He came back and lowered the gangplank, and we all stepped off.

"We won't be long," Braxton said to Wade.

"Take your time, sir."

We left the wharf and picked our way across a rocky beach before heading up a wide dirt pathway under a pretty canopy of trees. We were in dappled shade, and the air turned a few degrees cooler.

I could hear a roaring sound as we walked. "Is that the waterfall?" I asked.

"We're almost there," Braxton answered.

Just then, we rounded a bend and came to a picturesque little pool. It was surrounded by a beach of flat, smooth stones. The water was bright green, and a high waterfall fell on the opposite side, about fifty feet away, boiling the water into a white foam.

The faintest hint of spray reached us.

"Wow," was all I could say as I stared. Talk about a natural wonder.

"We'd bring the kids here when they were little," he said with a wistful tone and a faraway look in his eyes.

"Did Emily like it?" I asked, guessing that's where his thoughts had gone.

He nodded, then he bent down and picked up one of the stones. He slung it sideways, expertly skipping it over the water, five, six, seven times before it disappeared into the waterfall.

"You must miss her," I offered softly.

"Every day."

"I'm so sorry."

He shook his head. "None of this is remotely your fault." He gazed around. "But I wanted to show this to you. Because—" He shrugged his broad shoulders. "I don't know. I feel like you missed out on so much."

I could tell this was a special place for him, but I didn't know what more to say.

To my relief, his expression changed.

He looked meaningfully down at the gravel beach, a little grin growing on his face. "Give it a shot."

"Yeah?"

"It was a favorite pastime."

"Okay," I agreed with a grin of my own.

My first effort was a flop, and he chuckled. "More to the side, crouch and give it a little bit of an upswing."

He demonstrated, and I tried again.

I had more success this time, and by my tenth rock I was making it almost to the waterfall.

"I can see why you love it here," I said.

"It's a hidden gem. The looks of the wharf scares people off, so nobody's been inclined to upgrade it."

"Helps keep it a secret," I guessed, feeling like I was part of a secret society.

"We should head back," he said with a sigh, his expression turning sad for a moment. "I do have a conference call at noon."

"Thanks for showing this to me," I said, softening toward him even more.

"Anytime." He smiled again, and the wistful expression was back. Then he lobbed a final rock into the pond.

Ten

"He took you to Fiddler's Point?" Adeline asked from where she leaned on the doorjamb of my open bathroom door.

I'd showered the salt spray from my hair and changed my clothes.

"It was great," I said over the sound of the blow-dryer.

Stone had suggested dinner tonight, and I thought I might ask him about going sailing someday.

"We used to go there all the time when we were kids," Adeline said. "Have they rebuilt the dock?"

I shook my head. "Braxton said it was a disguise."

Adeline flashed a grin.

"We skipped rocks," I offered.

"That's a time-honored tradition." Adeline fell silent.

In the mirror, I caught a pensive expression on her face and shut off the blow-dryer. I turned to her. "What?"

"He's really pulling out all the stops with you." The wheels were obviously turning inside Adeline's head.

I knew she was perpetually suspicious of Braxton's motives. "Stone says Braxton feels guilty."

Adeline's eyes narrowed.

"For mixing me up at the hospital," I elaborated. "Like he should have recognized one newborn baby from another after only a few hours."

"Braxton's not motivated by guilt. I don't say that to be mean. He's just a very complex man."

"Complex, sure, but he did bring home the wrong baby daughter." I surprised myself with my blasé delivery of the statement.

The guilt angle seemed entirely plausible to me. It also struck me that he was trying to make up for lost time. Today had been fun in the end, but it had sure felt forced at the beginning.

Adeline nodded, although she didn't look completely convinced. But then she smiled. "Enough psychoanalyzing. What's up for the rest of the day?"

"Stone wants to go into town for dinner."

Adeline brightened. "Yeah? Where? Moonstone's? I'd be up for some dancing." She shuffled a couple of steps, then did a twirl.

I was pretty sure Stone was planning on it being just the two of us.

"I've got the perfect dress for you to borrow," Adeline continued, heading out of the bathroom.

I followed.

"Either the teal green with the little lace insets or the butter yellow off the shoulder," she said. "Hmm... Maybe not the yellow, maybe the basic black instead. It's got a little swirl in the skirt. The yellow's not the best if we're going to be eating. Oh, and I've got a *ton* of shoes you can pick from—some a little big for me, some a little small. We'll find you something."

She sounded so enthusiastic, that I didn't have the heart to tell her she couldn't come along. And why shouldn't she come along? Stone and I could still dance together. Dancing would be romantic.

"Sophie?" Stone's voice sounded outside my bedroom door as he rapped gently.

"Come on in," Adeline called out.

He did.

"I hear we're going to Moonstone's tonight," Adeline said. She glanced at her watch. "Sophie and I should start getting ready for that."

Stone shot me a look of confusion.

I gave a helpless little shrug in return.

"Moonstone's sounds good to me," Mason said appearing in the doorway behind Stone. "I'll let Kyle know."

I fought off a laugh at Stone's expression, but I didn't see how we could back out now. There was no choice but to roll with it.

By the time we all got ready and assembled in the front hall, it was coming up on seven. I'd gone with the teal dress, liking how the subtle lace on the bodice and at the midthigh hem gave a layered look to the fabric. Adeline went with the black. We both agreed yellow was too much of a risk, although it had looked amazing when she modeled it.

Stone wore casual slacks and a nicely cut sports jacket, while Mason and Kyle went with dress shirts alone. They all wore ties and looked very handsome. I had a feeling our table would get a lot of attention from the women in the room once the dancing started.

"What's happening here?" Braxton asked, looking us all up and down as he marched in from the great room.

"We're heading into town," Mason answered for the group.

"Did I miss something?" Xavier came up on us from the opposite direction, a newspaper under his arm.

"They're going to town," Braxton said. There was something meaningful in the look he gave his brother.

"Bit of a problem with that," Xavier said, moving forward.

"What problem?" Kyle asked.

"Family meeting tonight," Xavier said.

"For *what*?" Adeline asked, clearly frustrated.

"All of us?" Kyle asked.

"Just the three of you." Xavier's glance took in each of his kids.

"Not Stone?" Mason asked.

"It's an estate planning issue," Xavier said.

"Tonight?" Kyle seemed dumbfounded.

"Why tonight?" Mason asked.

"It can wait," Adeline said.

"The lawyers need it first thing in the morning. Filing issue."

"Are you serious?" Mason asked.

"Wouldn't be saying it if I wasn't serious." Xavier shrugged.

I looked at Stone, and he gave me a half smile. I could see what he was thinking. It was back to just the two of us.

I couldn't say I was massively disappointed in the turn of events, but I felt sorry for Adeline, Kyle and Mason, since they'd dressed up and were raring to go. But I'd take Stone alone any night of the week.

Braxton clapped Stone on the shoulder. "No need to mess up your plans."

Adeline gave a slow turn of her head to stare suspiciously at Braxton.

"Shall we?" Stone asked me.

"Sorry, guys," I said to the other three.

Kyle waved me off. Mason rolled his eyes. Adeline was the only one who looked truly bothered.

"Lesson time," Stone whispered as we made our way out the front door.

"Lesson on what? Tell me you didn't put Xavier up to that."

Stone looked genuinely surprised. "I did not. I wouldn't undermine Mason and the rest. Why would you think I'd do that?"

"Because you just said this was lesson time."

"Not a lesson on scheming. A lesson on being rich."

"Is that what we're doing?"

"You wanted to learn how to be rich."

"At Moonstone's?" I liked Moonstone's a lot. It was a great place. But it wasn't exactly upscale snooty.

"I still have a reservation for two at The Big Edge."

"Is that the snooty place?"

"It's gracious and classy—and very expensive."

"Then bring it on." I did want to hear Stone's take on being rich, since he hadn't been born with a silver spoon in his mouth. He'd barely been born with a spoon at all.

He steered me to a black SUV and opened the passenger door.

We left the SUV with the valet and crossed a pretty front porch covered in latticework, flowers, subtle white lights and glowing antique lamps positioned in a row along the floorboards.

"Step one," Stone said.

"Open the door?" I asked.

"Cute." He opened it. "Tip the valet well. He's probably putting himself through college, plus he'll take really good care of your vehicle."

"Is he putting himself through college?" I asked as I

stepped over the threshold. Stone obviously knew something about the young man since he'd called him by name.

"As a matter of fact, he's in engineering. We may end up hiring him at Kodiak when he graduates."

We entered a small, plain foyer, and Stone pressed the button for an elevator.

"We're going up?" I asked.

"We're going up."

The panel pinged and the button light went out as the elevator door slid open. Stone followed me inside, and it closed again.

"Alone at last," he said and slipped an arm around my waist.

All of me sighed in pleasure at his touch.

He moved so we were chest to chest. As the elevator rose, he cradled my cheek with his palm and placed a tender kiss on my lips. "I've missed that."

"Me too," I admitted, leaning into him. "Me too."

As we came to a smooth stop, he smiled and turned, keeping one hand loosely around my waist as we walked into the restaurant foyer.

"Good evening, Mr. Stone." A smartly dressed hostess stepped from behind a polished wood counter to greet us. She was tall, willowy with very long brunette hair. Her smile for Stone said she found him attractive.

Who could blame her? He was spectacular.

"Hi, Kristy," he replied. "How are you doing tonight?"

"I'm very well, thanks." She retrieved two leather-bound menus. "Your usual table?"

"Please."

As she turned into the dining room, I leaned close to Stone. "Is she in college too?"

"I don't know for sure. But I think she's a little old for college."

He was probably right. I'd have guessed she was in her late twenties.

We followed her through a subtly lighted dining room. It was Alaska rustic but in the finest of ways, polished wooden beams outlining wide windows with the glowing lights of the city beyond. The tables were well spaced, each with a mini antique lamp in the center with its light flickering a soft romantic yellow. The service entrances were disguised and well away from the dining area. The music was subtle, and the temperature perfect.

Kristy led us to a round table in a little alcove next to the windows.

The white linens were pressed. The silverware polished, and the china was fine white and gold, everything positioned exactly right.

Stone pulled out my chair, and I sat on a soft cushion, nestled in a curved wraparound back.

"Thanks, Kristy," he said as he moved to his chair.

If I hadn't been looking for it, I wouldn't have seen him slip her a folded bill. I knew hostesses at The Blue Fern were supported by the waitstaffs' tips. It was rare for them to receive tips of their own. I wondered if it was different in Alaska, different in an establishment this upscale or different because it was Stone.

"Does everybody do that?" I asked him.

He settled into the chair around the table curve from mine, both of us facing the window.

"Do what?"

"Hand out tips to everyone who moves. How much did you give the valet?"

"Enough," he said with a little smile.

"I'm supposed to be learning here."

Stone reached out and took my hand.

My attention shifted to his touch, and I almost forgot the question.

"This is a nice place," he said.

"I agree."

The Blue Fern was special, and I could tell this place was a leap above it.

"People come here often."

"Because of the food?"

"Because of the contribution to the local economy. The Big Edge charges high prices and pays higher wages, creating plum food sector jobs in Anchorage." He paused. "Don't get me wrong, it's not completely altruistic. I enjoy fine food and fine service. It's a happily symbiotic relationship."

"You have a nice evening and leave behind as much money as possible." That certainly made sense from a local economic perspective.

He rubbed his thumb across the back of my hand, raising goose bumps. "Go to the head of the class."

I struggled to keep my attention on the conversation instead of focusing solely on his touch. "Well, you gave me the CliffsNotes up front."

"I did."

"I don't know what we're going to do with the rest of the evening," I couldn't help teasing even as I glanced down to where he held my hand.

The waiter arrived, and Stone withdrew his touch.

"Good evening, Mr. Stone, ma'am."

"Good evening," I replied.

"Nice to see you again, Richard," Stone said.

"Can I start you off with a cocktail?"

Stone looked to me.

"Does the bartender have a specialty?" I was feeling

adventurous, plus I thought it was a good way to order an expensive drink.

"Indeed, he does. The Clear Glacier Martini."

"I'll try it," I said.

Stone gave me a knowing smile. "Same for me."

"Coming right up." Richard left the tableside.

"See, you catch on fast," Stone said with a smile.

"So, I did just order an expensive drink?"

"You did, and it's one of my favorites."

A second waiter arrived with a fragrant basket of rolls, setting them down with a flourish, then placing our cloth napkins in our laps before using silver tongs to put a roll on each of our bread plates.

"I try not to be the dead end." Stone tore his roll in half, and the delicious fragrance intensified.

"The place where the money stops circulating," I said with a nod. "My real problem is how to keep it moving on a large scale. I bought the biggest house I could reasonably live in by myself. And it's on some of the most expensive real estate in greater Seattle. I just bought a new vehicle here. I suppose I could buy a new car in Seattle, but that's where my imagination ends."

"In smaller economies like Alaska, jobs are the best way to keep the money train going."

"Kodiak Communications hires locally?"

"Anytime we can, and we support scholarships for hard-to-find skills."

"I don't want to open a business." The most obvious choice would be a restaurant. But I wasn't interested in getting back into that area, especially not as an owner. They were truly 24/7 operations. Plus, I felt like I should be moving forward not backward.

"Then find someone who does."

"You mean a partner?" I took a bite of my roll. It was

sweet and tender, the butter flavor bursting in my mouth. It was all I could do not to moan in appreciation. "These are fantastic."

"The head baker studied in France."

"Well, he…or she…sure learned a lot somewhere."

"I mean invest in a business," he said, digging into his own roll.

I'd never thought of myself as a venture capitalist, but maybe I should have. "That's what Jamie's company did for Sweet Tech, provided us with start-up capital."

"And that sure turned out well."

Our drinks arrived in chilled stemless martini glasses, crystal clear, just a touch of condensation and garnished with a swirl of lemon peel curving over the rim.

"I like it already," I said.

"Have a taste," Stone said, waiting for me.

I did. It was smooth, fresh and light. "Oh, yeah."

"Perfect," Stone said to the cocktail waitress.

I took another sip. "Braxton took me on the sailboat today."

Stone sipped his martini. "I heard."

"From Adeline?"

"From Braxton. It's been a while since he was out on the water."

"He took me to Fiddler's Point." I watched Stone's expression in the glowing lamplight, wondering if he'd question Braxton's motives like Adeline had.

But he didn't react at all. "It's nice out there. Good destination for a short trip. Had you ever sailed before?"

"No."

"What did you think? Some people don't like the motion."

"I was fine with it. I liked it a lot. I'd go again." I let the idea hang, thinking my hint was suitably subtle.

Hand on his glass, his smile widened. "I'll take you anytime."

"Braxton said you sailed."

"So that *was* a hint."

I lifted my glass for another sip. "Maybe."

"So, you're up for another date?" This time it was Stone gauging my expression.

"*Maybe*," I said on a teasing note. I let my eyes tell him I was completely up for another date.

He took my free hand with his. "Not that this one has to end anytime soon."

"Are we stretching it into dessert?"

"Dessert's a good idea. But we're sitting on top of an illustrious boutique hotel."

I reflexively glanced at the floor.

Stone leaned in and lowered his voice. "And we can stay here just as long as you like."

I liked. I truly did.

We opted for dessert in a hotel suite, ordering a bottle of champagne and a tray of decadent chocolate truffles.

The room service beat us to the suite, so while I toed off my shoes—well Adeline's shoes, black high slim-heeled pumps with inset crystals around the peekaboo toes—Stone extracted the champagne bottle from the ice bucket, removed the foil and popped the cork.

The living room had a modern feel to it, sleek leather furniture, warm cream-colored walls and a deep burgundy rug in front of a long glass fireplace set between the living room and the bedroom. A gas fire flickered low inside. The curtains were open on a floor-to-ceiling window overlooking the city.

My teal cocktail dress was pretty but not super comfortable, so I checked the bathroom and found a plush white robe, exchanging it with the dress and tightening the sash.

When I walked back into the living room, Stone froze in place, a glass of champagne in each hand. "You…look…"

"Comfortable?"

"Sexy. Beautiful. Desirable." He came my way. "How do you expect me to drink champagne while you're dressed like that?"

"Because it's very fine champagne." I took one of the glasses from his hand and took a sip. "And those truffles look like they're to die for."

I strolled to the dining table, where the truffles were set out on a silver tray. Their chocolate shells were beautifully colored, swirls of gold and purple, deep blue and ruby red. I went with a mottled purple, brought it to my lips and bit down.

I could feel Stone watching me. I felt sexy under his gaze, aroused by passion but in no hurry to rush through it.

"Oh, that's good," I said, turning to share my expression of bliss.

He joined me, and I held out the other half of the truffle. "Taste?"

He took the chocolate in his mouth, sucking on my fingers.

Desire shimmered through me, increasing, intensifying as he drew closer, kissing me with his sweet mouth, easing me against him, letting our heat mingle.

I felt him remove the champagne glass from my hand. I didn't know where he put it, and I didn't care, because he tugged on the sash of my robe, unfastening it, pushing aside the fabric, slipping his hands inside the folds and wrapping his arms around me.

I tipped my head and kissed him more deeply.

His palm slipped around my waist, moving up, covering my bare breast.

"The champagne can wait," he growled.

I agreed. Everything could wait. There was nothing in the world more important than making love with Stone.

He scooped me into his arms and headed for the bedroom, tossing back the covers and laying me down on the cool crisp sheets.

I waited there in anticipation, watching while he stripped off his jacket and tie, his shirt and slacks. His gaze stayed fixed on me until he was naked. Then he knelt down and slowly peeled my panties down my thighs, my calves, over my ankles.

His kissed his way back, taking his time, pausing at my belly, my breasts, my neck and my lips. And then he was on top of me. Our kisses and caresses turned to a tangle of arms and legs.

We were together again, and the waves and pangs of passion I was coming to love swept between us. I didn't want it to end, but the force was unstoppable. We climbed higher and higher, holding out and hanging on until the last second when we cried out our passion and crested together in waves of unremitting pleasure.

I felt myself drop back to earth in stages.

Stone's weight pinned me down, hot with a sheen of sweat between our bodies.

The sheets were cool where I stretched out my arms but warm right under me.

We were sideways on the bed with a ceiling fan above us. Its blades were still, but shimmers of heat from the gas fireplace wafted our way. The orange light flickered on the walls and reflected off the massive window.

Stone rose on his elbows to look at me.

I gazed back. I didn't have anything to say. I didn't feel the need to speak.

"You're amazing," he finally said into the silence.

I couldn't stop myself from smiling in absolute joy. "You're not so bad yourself."

"I mean it, Sophie. This is…" He shifted to one side. His fingertip traced my face. "I've never felt like this before."

I hadn't either. I didn't know what to make of it. I knew I was falling for Stone. I was falling fast and hard and maybe irrevocably. But I didn't have any context for my feelings.

I turned my head to look at him. "I've never felt like this either."

"Good," he said. Then he leaned forward for a tender kiss.

For some reason, it nearly brought me to tears. Emotion clogged my chest. I couldn't seem to talk, so I wrapped my arms around his neck and held him close for long minutes.

"Thirsty?" he whispered in my ear.

"Sure." I couldn't think of anything better than to lie here in bed and sip champagne.

He eased back from me and rolled to his feet, walking naked into the living room and returning with the champagne and the truffles as well. He set a glass on my bedside table, and I pulled up to sitting, arranging the pillows to lean on. There were eight of them, so I tossed a couple across the room to get them out of the way.

Stone laughed at that and climbed in the other side, setting the truffles between us.

"I'm glad we kept our priorities straight," he said as he took a truffle then popped it into his mouth.

"Was there ever any doubt?" I asked.

"That the minute we found ourselves alone together we'd hop into bed?" He finished my thought. "No. No doubt about that."

We looked at each other and smiled. Whatever else was going on here, the sex was fantastic. Why wouldn't we want to do it as soon and as often as possible?

Stone's phone rang from the pocket of his jacket tossed on an armchair beside the window.

"You should get that," I said.

"They'll call back."

"You sure? You don't even want to check?"

"I'm sure. No, I don't want to check. I want to lay here naked with you and drink champagne."

"Good choice."

"Thank you, ma'am."

"Do you think *ma'am* makes me sound old?"

Stone cocked his head in astonishment. "What? You're nowhere near old."

"The waiter called me that too."

"He was just being polite." Stone paused. "I was being amusing."

"Oh." I struggled to keep a straight face. "I didn't get that."

He nudged me with his shoulder as I reached for a truffle, making me fumble.

"Hey," I admonished him. "Don't get between me and my dessert."

"You have a sweet tooth?"

"Big-time. You?"

He shrugged. "I like rich more than I do sweet, like dark chocolate and cream."

"Well, buck up, man. These are pretty sweet."

He lifted a red swirled chocolate to size it up. "I know."

"Or back off and let me eat them."

"All of them?"

"Maybe not *all* of them. We can order you something else."

"I'm manly enough to make the sacrifice." He popped the chocolate into his mouth.

His phone rang again, and he heaved a sigh.

"Better check," I said. "It might be important."

"Nothing's more important than you."

"Maybe a cell tower blew up or got struck by lightning. Maybe the whole Alaska grid is down, and they need you to do disaster coordination."

"Then how are they calling me?"

"I don't know." I nodded to the sound of the ringtone. "Ask them and find out."

He rolled his eyes at me but went for the phone.

"Yeah?" He paused and looked my way. "Can that question not wait?" He listened, then frowned. "Right." He gave me a shake of his head, then pointed to the bedroom door.

I nodded. It did seem like something had gone wrong.

He left and closed the door behind him.

I sat for a second, finishing another truffle. But then I remembered my own phone was in the en suite where I'd left it when I put on the robe.

I retrieved it and called Tasha.

"Finally." She sounded happy as she answered.

"Sorry about that."

"Are you still sailing?"

"No. No. That ended earlier today. I got caught up with Adeline, one of the other cousins."

"I remember."

"Then…Stone and I decided to go out for dinner. I mean, well, we were all going to—"

"You're with Stone?"

"Yes."

"Right now?"

"Uh-huh."

"What are you doing talking to me? Hang up already and get back to the hunk."

"I didn't say he was a hunk."

"I have access to social media. You don't think I did a search on him?"

"Okay, yeah, he's a hunk. He's also in the other room on a call."

Tasha's tone changed. "I thought you were out for dinner."

"We were. We kind of still are. But we moved dessert to a hotel suite."

"Way to go, *Sophie*." There was a smile in her voice. "So, you like him a lot."

"I do." I plopped my head back down on the pillow. "I'm… I don't know… Thing is… I mean, he's just so…"

"Oh, my." Tasha sounded amazed.

"Yeah."

"You've fallen hard."

"I don't know what hard feels like, but this is something. I wish you could meet him. You'd see what I mean."

"So, bring him home. We'll come to Seattle for a visit." There was a muffled sound in the background on Tasha's end of the phone. "It's Sophie," she called to whoever was with her. "There's a guy." Then she was back to me. "Jamie says hi."

"Tell him hi back." I pictured introducing Stone to Tasha and Jamie. They'd like him. I knew they would.

The bedroom door opened, and Stone reappeared in all his naked glory.

"Gotta go," I said to Tasha.

She laughed at me. "You bet."

Eleven

Stone and I barely stopped at the mansion the next morning, just long enough to change into casual clothes. From there, we went to the marina and hopped on the sailboat. Wade wasn't working, but Stone sailed us off for a glorious day together.

We headed along the shoreline while Stone taught me the basics of sailing. I was klutzy, but we laughed a lot. Then we stopped at a little village, ate lunch and bought some baked goods for the boat. We bought some souvenirs, silly out-of-season things like mittens and scarves to help clear the inventory of a little store. Then we loaded everything into the sailboat, heading for home, stopping for a tryst in a deserted cove before docking back at the marina.

Adeline was in my bedroom minutes after I got there.

"You two stayed out all night," she said.

I couldn't keep the satisfied smirk from my face. "We did."

I expected a grin in return and was surprised when she frowned instead.

"What?" I asked her.

"Last night was a setup." She plunked down on the end of my bed.

She had me confused. "A setup how?"

"My dad didn't need to keep us here last night." She waved a dismissive hand through the air. "I mean, sure he had some document, and he made a big deal about the fact that Braxton had a new heir now."

I stiffened. "An heir?" I didn't like the sound of that. "You don't mean me."

"Sure, I mean you."

My buoyant mood slipping a little, I sat down on the other end of the bed. "I'm not Braxton's heir."

Adeline blinked at me in obvious disbelief. "Yeah, you are."

"I'm not. I mean biologically, sure. But I'm not inter-ested in inheriting anything from him." Deciding I was his heir seemed way over-the-top at this point. We were barely getting to know each other.

"Braxton's going to do what Braxton's going to do," Adeline said. "But that's not my point."

I thought it was a pretty important point.

"We're years," she continued, "I mean *years* away from any of that mattering. The idea that Mason, Kyle and I had to stay home last night to deal with it is ridiculous. So, you know…"

I tried to read her expression. "I know what?"

"It was definitely a *setup*, Sophie."

"*What* was a setup?" I felt like we were going around in circles.

"Last night. You and Stone. Braxton's throwing you together with Stone."

"Stone was the one who asked me on a date."

Adeline was nodding to herself. "It's all starting to come together now."

"Stone asked me out a couple days ago," I explained. "It was all planned before last night." As the words came out, I realized that sounded like she'd been unwelcome. "Don't get me wrong, I didn't mind the idea of you guys coming along."

Adeline came to her feet and took a couple of paces. "Braxton loves Stone like a son. And now here you are, his daughter." She held her palms open as if her conclusion was obvious.

"You're saying Braxton wants me to get together with Stone."

"*Yes!* I was vaguely suspicious before, but now I'm positive."

I didn't want to burst Adeline's bubble, but if Stone and I weren't attracted to each other, there was nothing Braxton could do to force the situation. We were attracted to each other, but it had absolutely nothing to do with Braxton.

"You do know Braxton has no control over my emotions, or Stone's emotions, or anybody's emotions for that matter."

She returned to the bed and sat back down. From her faraway expression, I wasn't sure if she'd heard me.

"He needed the rest of us to stay home so that you two could be alone together."

"What if he did?" I wasn't really seeing that it mattered much.

Adeline peered at me as if I was missing some important point. "That's his superpower."

"Superpower?" I was thinking of Stone now, and the options for declaring he had a superpower—intelligence, looks, sense of humor, strength, compassion. The list was long.

"Braxton's superpower. My dad's too. They have a way of making you think it's all your idea."

I fought the urge to laugh at that. "It takes more than ESP to get me into bed with a man."

"But you did go to bed with Stone."

"I did."

"I rest my case."

I still struggled not to grin at the absurdity of her theory. "I slept with Stone because I like him. I like him a lot."

I was beginning to suspect I liked Stone more than just a lot, but I wasn't ready to share that detail with Adeline, at least not yet and definitely not during this conversation.

"I can see now that Braxton wants little Stone and Sophie babies to perpetuate his dynasty," she continued as if I hadn't spoken. "I can only imagine he's over the moon at the thought of it."

"It's not Braxton's decision," I pointed out again.

I might like Stone a lot, but it was far, far too early to think about making babies with him. I pushed the idea firmly from my head.

Adeline leaned forward. "All I'm saying is don't lose yourself."

"I'm not losing myself. How would I be losing myself?"

"This." She waved her arm in an arc. "It's always been so big."

"The place is huge." I had to agree with that.

"More than just the house," she said. "The family, the dynasty. It's easy to get swept up in the drama and grandeur of it all. Braxton wants you to stay in Alaska for his own reasons. But don't forget who you are."

I wasn't sure how to take that. "I know who I am."

Okay, so I might not have figured out everything about being rich Sophie. But I wasn't about to fall into line with whatever Alaskan plans my biological father might have for me.

Braxton might want my life to work out the way Adeline described. But he couldn't force me to do things I didn't want to do.

"I've insulted you," she said, looking contrite.

"No, no." She hadn't, not really.

She couldn't know me well enough to realize I was clear thinking and emotionally grounded. I'd always been grounded. It might be my personal superpower.

"I'm sorry," she said.

I reached out to squeeze her hand. "You have nothing to be sorry about. You're watching out for me."

She squeezed my hand in return. "You're my cousin."

I smiled at that as I let her go, feeling really good about our relationship.

"We women have to stick together," she finished.

"We will," I agreed, meaning it.

She paused then. "I do know you're smart. I do know you're logical. Just promise me you'll keep your head in the game."

"I'll keep my head in the game."

"And don't take anything at face value."

I started to smile again. "I like Stone," I repeated. "I like him a lot, and it has nothing to do with Braxton."

She looked like she wanted to say more, but she pressed her lips together instead. "Spit it out," I told her.

She shook her head. "I've said too much already."

"We're cousins," I pointed out. "We share."

She took a breath. "Just make sure..." She hesitated again. "Make sure you put yourself...your wants, your needs first. Don't get swept away by the family's aspirations."

"I can do that." I knew I could. I wasn't about to let Braxton or anyone else mess with my head.

I headed downstairs for dinner, my path taking me through the great room toward the kitchen and the informal dining area where the family usually ate. I couldn't help looking forward to seeing Stone, but I warned myself to keep my expression neutral. I didn't want Braxton or anyone else to guess at the off-the-charts chemistry between us.

I heard Stone's voice first, deep and resonant from the den. His words were indistinct, but I felt the vibration right down to my toes and instinctively moved closer.

Braxton answered him back. "I don't think you are, Stone. I really don't think you are." He sounded annoyed, like he had back that first day I'd met him.

The surprise slowed my steps.

"I've done everything you asked." There was an edge to Stone's voice too.

"You're dragging your feet. You don't think I can't see you're dragging your feet?"

"We're not making widgets here."

I took a backward step. I didn't know what they were fighting about, but it was none of my business.

Braxton gave a cold laugh. "She already likes you."

I paused. She?

"I'm not pushing any harder." Stone's voice was resolute.

"I'm not asking you to push harder."

"That's exactly what you're asking me to do."

"I'm asking you to see the opportunities, exploit the opportunities."

"Exploit?" Stone asked.

"Maybe that was the wrong word."

There was a beat of silence in the room.

"You're too impatient," Stone said.

I glanced to the staircase then, knowing Adeline was still up there. Her earlier words echoed, and I was horribly afraid I was the "she" in question—the one who liked Stone and wasn't being properly exploited.

"You're telling me this is the best you can do?" Braxton asked.

"I'm telling you to *back off.*"

"We're on the clock."

"She's always going to be your daughter."

I felt my knees go weak.

Braxton's voice softened. "But she's not always going to be here."

"Under your control."

"Available. You know how these things go. Close the deal, Stone. Close it now."

They were silent for a long while.

"I owe you." Stone's voice had turned low and thick. "I will always owe you. For what you did, for what I did, for what you forgave, but I have my limits."

A whimper escaped me, and I put my fingertips to my lips. The last thing I needed was for them to catch me listening.

I couldn't let them discover me out here.

I couldn't face either of them ever again.

"You owe me," Braxton agreed as I took a step back, poised to flee.

"But I won't lie to her," Stone said.

I almost laughed at that one, a hysterical laugh, a desperate laugh. It seemed like Stone had done nothing but lie to me all along.

He'd done everything Braxton asked. He'd just said so

himself. And it was obvious Braxton had asked him to snare me in a romance.

An image of lying naked in Stone's arms came up in my mind—naked and smiling, as if all was well with the world.

I ruthlessly tamped it down.

"Just one more step," Braxton said.

"Not right now. Not like this." Stone was emphatic.

"The grandchildren," Braxton said, a catch to his voice. "*My* grandchildren."

"I'm not saying never."

I pressed my fingertips harder against my lips. Did Stone think stringing me along even longer was somehow an answer? Did he plan to keep wooing me until…until I—

My breath left my body, and my heart sank to my toes.

"You can't let this chance slip past," Braxton said.

A voice shouted inside my head as I backed farther away. I would *not* fall in love with Stone. Not now, not ever.

Stone spoke again, but his voice was indistinct as I made it to the staircase. I rushed silently up and into my room, pulling my suitcase out of the closet and opening it on the bed.

I grabbed shirts and jeans and underwear out of the dresser drawers, tossing them haphazardly into the case.

"Sophie?" Adeline walked in through the open balcony door. "What?" Her eyes widened as I tossed my toiletries into the suitcase and zipped it shut.

"You were right," I told her, stopping for a deep breath. My lungs hurt. My chest hurt. My throat felt raw and dry.

"About what?" she asked, looking stricken now.

"Everything. Him, them." I gestured vaguely out the door. "I have to go. Now. Right now."

"Oh, no." She took a step closer, reaching out to me.

"I overheard." My voice quaked. "Them." My emotions were a jumble, and I was afraid to try to sort them out.

Adeline drew me into a hug. "I'm so sorry."

"He was pretending all along, Adeline." I pulled back. "They were planning, scheming about a future for us."

She rubbed my upper arms. "They can't help themselves."

"I have to go." I backed away.

"I know."

"Stone lied straight to my—" I couldn't finish. I couldn't put into words how badly I felt betrayed. I slung my purse over my shoulder.

"Wait," she said. "How did Stone—"

"I should have listened to you." I pulled the suitcase from the bed and started for the door. "I'll text. I'll call." Maybe Adeline could visit me in Seattle, or I could hop down to California. It wasn't like money would be an object.

"Sophie, wait—"

But I couldn't wait any longer. I had to get out of here before I ran into Stone.

"You're going to love it here," Tasha said with patently forced enthusiasm.

We were sitting in my new living room on unfamiliar sofas picked by a decorator to coordinate with her choice of landscape paintings, everything positioned to highlight my new million-dollar water view. It was obscured by a downpour right now, but the rain suited my mood.

Tasha and her husband, Jamie, had flown up from California this morning as soon as I told her why I'd left Alaska. Jamie had braved the rain on a wine and pizza run an hour ago. We were drinking merlot from my old wineglasses. At least those were familiar and a little bit comforting.

"Eventually," I dutifully agreed with her statement.

"I can talk to you about heartbreak," Jamie said, resettling himself in one of the armchairs. "And humiliation." He was referring to the day his bride, Brooklyn, had left him at the altar. He then sent a smile Tasha's way. "And about getting your happily-ever-after when you least expect it."

"Too soon, honey," Tasha said with a meaningful look toward me.

"Yeah," Jamie agreed. "Sorry, Sophie. Just go ahead and drink up. There's another bottle if we need it. I also picked up a few pints of mocha almond fudge."

"You're the best," I said, managing a smile. I'd been teary-eyed most of the day, but talking things out with Tasha had helped, and Jamie had been empathetic too.

There was a sharp knock on the front door, and we all looked at each other in surprise.

"No one knows I live here," I said.

"A neighbor?" Tasha guessed.

"In this rain?"

"Maybe there's some kind of emergency. I'll go check." Jamie rolled to his feet and headed for the foyer.

I heard the door open. Then I heard Stone's voice. It was unmistakable.

Tasha caught my shocked expression. Her eyes went round. "Is that *him*?"

I reflexively pressed my back against the sofa. "Make him go away."

"You bet I will." Tasha was on her feet and crossing the room.

"Wait." I stopped her.

She turned, and we stared at each other for a moment.

I didn't want to see him. Did I?

"Sophie?" Jamie appeared. "He's insisting—"

"Please hear me out," Stone said to me. He'd followed Jamie into the living room.

Jamie turned to face him, folding his arms over his chest, widening his stance as he blocked Stone.

"It's okay," I said to Jamie, secretly relieved to have the decision taken out of my hands.

Maybe this confrontation had to happen. Maybe it would help me to move on.

"You sure?" Jamie asked over his shoulder.

"I'm sure."

Jamie stayed put for a second longer, then, seeming reluctant, moved to one side.

Stone's gaze met mine. Energy shot between us, storming my emotional barriers, bringing back every glorious minute we'd spent together.

"Can we talk?" he asked, glancing around like he wanted some privacy.

"Say it here." I didn't trust myself to be alone with him.

He looked at Jamie's scowling face and then at Tasha, who was obviously more than ready to jump to my defense.

He heaved a sigh of capitulation. "Adeline told me what happened."

I managed an indifferent shrug. It wasn't like he didn't already know what he'd done. Adeline didn't need to clue him in on that.

He took a couple of steps toward me, glancing sidelong at Jamie. "You walked out."

I nodded sharply.

Adeline might have clued him in, or maybe he'd made an educated guess. But his guilty expression said he knew that I knew.

"You should have come talk to me."

I raised my brow. "Seriously? So you could lie to me some more?"

He canted his head. "So I could tell you the truth."

I gave a cold laugh. "What truth?"

"That when you walked out that door, my heart left with you."

I wasn't about to let him get away with that statement. "We both know that's not true."

"Sophie, you don't know how I feel."

"I know what you did. I know what you want. I know you *owed* Braxton."

He drew up straight. "This isn't about Braxton."

I came to my feet. "From what I overheard, *everything's* about Braxton."

Stone's voice stayed level and calm. "You don't know as much as you think you do."

"I know enough." The jig was up already. I couldn't figure out what he was doing here. It wasn't like I'd fall for his lies all over again, swoon and fall into his arms.

"I'll leave Alaska," Stone stated.

The words stopped me cold.

"We can stay in Seattle," he continued. "Or we can go someplace else, anywhere you want."

I didn't believe him, not for a second. Braxton would never let that happen, so it had to be another trick, another way to manipulate me.

"How would that work?" I pressed, forcing him to admit it was a ruse.

He looked baffled for a second. "The usual way."

I wasn't letting him gloss over whatever it was he was saying. "What's the usual way?"

"I stay here." He looked around himself. "Or we buy a house someplace else. I'm very employable in the tech sector. We'd have options."

Now I was the one who was baffled. Was Stone offering to give up his life in Alaska for Braxton's dream of grandchildren?

What then?

Would we take the kids to Alaska for occasional visits? I doubted Braxton would be satisfied with that arrangement.

"I need you, Sophie," Stone said, reaching into his pocket.

"For what?" I was trying, but I wasn't seeing his endgame here.

He produced a small velvet box and popped it open to reveal a solitaire diamond. "Forever."

For a split second, my heart took him seriously, and I wanted to throw myself into his arms. But then I remembered Braxton's plea to Stone: just one more step.

This was obviously that step.

I squared my shoulders, forcibly hardening my heart. "You'd actually *marry me* to make him happy?"

Stone looked aghast. "This isn't about him."

"Everything's about him. It's been about him from minute one."

"Sophie, no—"

"Give it up, Stone. You were caught out. It's over."

Stone's voice got deeper, more determined. "Okay, yes, I'm loyal to Braxton. And yes, he threw us together. And I let him. But I liked you. I liked you a lot."

"Well, wasn't that lucky for you."

"Sophie."

"Don't Sophie me. What kind of man—"

"You were *there*," Stone blurted. "Do you think I was *faking* it?"

His reserve seemed spent. Instead, he seemed to be running on pure emotion. In answer to his question, I didn't know. I would have bet not. But I hadn't seen the con coming either.

"I *owe* Braxton," Stone said, his jaw tight. "More than I can ever repay. And, at first, that was part of my motivation."

"I know he took you in." Knowing what I did, I couldn't truly blame Stone for his gratitude to Braxton.

"Took me in?" Stone gave a hoarse laugh. "That's not the half of it. He let me *stay*."

I already knew the foster care story.

"After I killed her," Stone finished flatly.

My knees went weak, and I gripped the back of a chair.

"It was my fault Emily died," Stone said with cold, hard finality. "I was supposed to drive that day, but I was goofing off with my friends. Christine hated driving on the icy roads. She hated—" He seemed to stagger for a second.

My heart went out to him. "Oh, Stone."

"And then you showed up. And it was a second chance. He asked for my help, at first just to keep you there so he could get to know you. But then he saw us together, and he thought about what might be. He started picturing grandchildren." Stone paused, but none of the rest of us broke the silence. "It was the first time in eighteen years I'd seen him truly, unreservedly happy."

"You can't marry me for Braxton." I didn't care how much Stone owed the man.

"I'm not marrying you for Braxton. I want you for me. I love you, Sophie. I've loved you since we faced down that bear."

"I don't believe you." How could I? He was faking it for Braxton, again for Braxton. Everything was for Braxton.

"Do you love me, Sophie?"

"No." My lie was quick and sharp.

Stone stared at me a minute longer. It felt like he was

daring me to tell the truth. But then his expression changed. He looked defeated. He snapped the ring box shut, turned and walked out the door.

It closed behind him to silence, nothing but the rain pounding on the roof, splattering on the deck outside.

"That was…" Tasha was the first to speak.

"He seemed…" Jamie looked at Tasha.

"It was like that the whole time," I said.

They both looked at me, clearly puzzled.

"Adeline warned me not to trust anything. They are the most complicated family."

"All families are complicated," Jamie said.

Tasha nodded. "Jamie's sister married his ex-fiance's husband's twin brother."

"Complicated," Jamie said with a nod.

"That was different," I said.

"Different how?" Tasha asked.

"Max was in love with Layla."

Jamie's gaze turned to my front foyer. "That guy… I'd say that guy's got it very bad for you, Sophie."

As Jamie voiced it, I knew it was true and my heart sank.

Stone had just proposed. He'd told me he loved me. He was loyal to Braxton, sure. But I knew about their scheme. Why would he still lie about loving me?

"Oh, no," I said out loud.

"Go," Tasha said.

I rushed for the door, out into the rain, where my blouse was instantly wet to my skin.

Stone was still there in the driveway, standing still, staring at the door of his rental car.

"Stone?"

He looked my way, his expression stark.

I kept moving forward. "I lied, Stone. I'm sorry. I love you. I love you so much."

He stared a moment longer, as if he didn't quite believe I was real.

Then he swallowed and opened his arms. I launched myself into them, feeling their strength close around me, feeling the warmth of his chest and the cool of the rain, on my head, in my hair, dripping down my face.

He kissed me hard, spinning me around. "Oh, Sophie."

He set me down slowly, then he reached into his pocket. He got down on one knee, ignoring the puddles, ignoring the driving rain. "Sophie, please, will you be my wife, have kids with me and make me the happiest man in the world?"

"Yes, Stone, oh, yes!" My heart sang with joy.

He rose, grinning, and slipped the ring on my finger. I stared down at the wet diamond sparkling under the driveway lights.

He looked past me and gave a nod. "Your friends."

I turned to see Tasha and Jamie, arm in arm, their smiles beaming at our happiness.

"We want to hear about the bear," Tasha called.

"Later," I said and flashed the ring.

They gave a cheer as I turned into Stone's arms.

"I'm a little afraid of that guy," Stone said into my ear.

I laughed at the thought of Stone being afraid of anyone or anything for that matter.

"We should go back to Alaska," I said.

"We can go anywhere you want."

"I want to spend time with Adeline and Mason and Kyle."

"And—" Stone hesitated. "Braxton?"

I gave a deep sigh. "Families are complicated."

"I don't know what that means."

"It means Braxton is my father, even if we do need to work out some boundaries."

"He'll be so thrilled to see you. He's heartsick about chasing you away."

"I'm sorry I bolted so fast."

"Don't be sorry."

"I should have stayed and fought…for us, for you, for my complicated family."

"You don't have to fight for me," Stone whispered, wrapping me close to his chest and his heart. "I fight for you. I love you, and I'm yours forever."

* * * * *

For more romances from award-winning author
Barbara Dunlop and Harlequin Desire,
visit www.Harlequin.com today!

**WE HOPE YOU ENJOYED
THIS BOOK FROM**

♦ HARLEQUIN

DESIRE

*Luxury, scandal, desire—welcome to
the lives of the American elite.*

Be transported to the worlds of oil barons, family dynasties,
moguls and celebrities. Get ready for juicy plot twists,
delicious sensuality and intriguing scandal.

6 NEW BOOKS AVAILABLE EVERY MONTH!

#2857 THE REBEL'S RETURN

Texas Cattleman's Club: Fathers and Sons • by Nadine Gonzalez

Eve Martin has one goal—find her nephew's father—and her unlikely ally is hotelier Rafael Wentworth, who's just returned to Texas and the family who abandoned him. Soon she's falling hard for the playboy in spite of their differences...and their secrets.

#2858 SECRETS OF A BAD REPUTATION

Dynasties: DNA Dilemma • by Joss Wood

Musician Griff O'Hare uses his bad-boy persona to keep others at bay. But when he's booked by straitlaced Kinga Ryder-White for her family's gala, he can't ignore their attraction. Yet as they fall for one another, everything around them falls apart...

#2859 HUSBAND IN NAME ONLY

Gambling Men • by Barbara Dunlop

Everyone believes ambitious Adeline Cambridge and rugged Alaskan politician Joe Breckenridge make a good match. So after one unexpected night and a baby on the way, their families push them into marriage. But will the convenient arrangement withstand the sparks and secrets between them?

#2860 EVER AFTER EXES

Titans of Tech • by Susannah Erwin

Dating app creator Will Taylor makes happily-ever-afters but remains a bachelor after his heart was broken by Finley Smythe. Reunited at a remote resort, they strike an uneasy truce after being stranded together. The attraction's still there even as their complicated past threatens everything...

#2861 ONE NIGHT CONSEQUENCE

Clashing Birthrights • by Yvonne Lindsay

As the widow of his best friend, Stevie Nickerson should be off-limits to CEO Fletcher Richmond, but there's a spark neither can ignore. When he learns she's pregnant, he insists on marriage, but Stevie relishes her independence. Can the two make it work?

#2862 THE WEDDING DARE

Destination Wedding • by Katherine Garbera

After learning a life-shattering secret, entrepreneur Logan Bisset finds solace in the arms of his ex, Quinn Murray. Meeting again at a Nantucket wedding, the heat's still there. But he might lose her again if he can't put the past behind him...

HDCNM0122B

"Hey, aren't you going to join me?" Paige asked, pushing wet hair back from her face and treading water in the center of the pool. "Swimming is on my list of fun things. We might as well kick things off with a bang."

Bang? Why had she said that? Lust immediately took over his senses. Desire beyond madness consumed him. He was determined that by the time they parted ways at the end of the month their sexual needs, wants and desires would be fulfilled and under control.

Quickly removing his shirt, Jess's hands went to his zipper, inched it down and slid the pants, along with his briefs, down his legs. He knew Paige was watching him and he was glad that he was the man she wanted.

"Come here, Paige."

She smiled and shook her head. "If you want me, Jess, you have to come and get me." She then swam to the far end of the pool, away from him.

Oh, so now she wanted to play hard to get? He had no problem going after her. Maybe now was a good time to tell her that not only had he been captain of his dog sled team, but he'd also been captain of his college swim team.

He glided through the water like an Olympic swimmer going after the gold, and it didn't take long to reach her. When she saw him getting close, she laughed and swam to the other side. Without missing a stroke or losing speed, he did a freestyle flip turn and reached out and caught her by the ankles. The capture was swift and the minute he touched her, more desire rammed through him to the point where water couldn't cool him down.

"I got you," he said, pulling her toward him and swimming with her in his arms to the edge of the pool.

When they reached the shallow end, he allowed her to stand, and the minute her feet touched the bottom she circled her arms around his neck. "No, Jess, I got you and I'm ready for you." Then she leaned in and took his mouth.

Don't miss what happens next in…
What Happens on Vacation…
by Brenda Jackson, the next book in her
Westmoreland Legacy: The Outlaws series!

Available March 2022 wherever
Harlequin Desire books and ebooks are sold.

Harlequin.com

Love Harlequin romance?

DISCOVER.

Be the first to find out about promotions,
news and exclusive content!

Facebook.com/HarlequinBooks

Twitter.com/HarlequinBooks

Instagram.com/HarlequinBooks

Pinterest.com/HarlequinBooks

YouTube.com/HarlequinBooks

ReaderService.com

EXPLORE.

Sign up for the Harlequin e-newsletter and
download a free book from any series at
TryHarlequin.com

CONNECT.

Join our Harlequin community to
share your thoughts and connect
with other romance readers!
Facebook.com/groups/HarlequinConnection